HIDDEN

FROM THE EDGE

BOOK FIVE

BY EVIE RILEY

HIDDEN

Can he learn to trust a stranger when all he's known is pain?

Eli might have escaped the conversion camp with his life, but now he's trapped inside his own head. Eli and his brother, Mia, are left to fend for themselves in a world that does not accept them. With no other choice, the two are forced to live in an abandoned warehouse.

Plagued by the complications of PTSD, finding a job isn't easy for Eli. He knows they've struck bottom when Mia turns to prostitution, and the guilt is eating him alive. This isn't the way their freedom was supposed to work. Hopelessness threatens to consume Eli, until he meets someone who offers to help.

Dr. Alex Howard comes across Eli suffering a major panic attack in the bathroom at an event in the hospital. Frustrated at his colleague's lazy treatment of the young man, Alex is convinced Eli needs a friend. He sets out to help boost the younger man's confidence, and to help him heal.

He doesn't expect to develop feelings for Eli, and though he's technically not crossing any boundaries, Alex is hesitant to act on his attraction.

Will Eli be able to move beyond his past? And can the two find romance in the process?

CHAPTER ONE

Eli

THESE PAST TWO months have not been easy on me. When I was trapped in the conversion camp, all I could think about was escaping the hell. After two and a half years, I never expected to be able to get out before my eighteenth birthday, which was a week ago, but I was finally free.

Craig Brooks, the evil piece of work who ran the camp, had finally made a fatal mistake by taking the wrong boy. A boy who had a brother that loved him very much and refused to allow him to be taken to a camp that would brainwash and condition him.

Now, over two hundred of us were finally free from the camp and it'd been shut down. The life of hell was over... or so I'd thought.

Unfortunately, the true reality of my situation has finally hit me. My freedom didn't come with leaving those walls. I was still trapped, but instead of cement walls that kept me in, it was my own mind.

Everyday was a challenge for me to be able to function. I was struggling with sleeping. I was struggling with being around people. I was struggling with being touched. I was a mess, and I was trapped in that hell in my own head.

So many of the other guys got to go somewhere. They got to go to a family member or to a foster home where they were safe. But me, my aunt was supposed to come and get me, but she never showed.

People didn't know that, but no one really asked, either. They just assumed she came and got me like she said she would. Only, when she didn't show, I was left with nothing all over again. I had no family. Well, I had my brother, but that was different. That wasn't a loving adult who would be there for me. I was still older than him, so it was on me to try and take care of him.

Which is what brought me to the

mall. I was determined to put it all behind me and get a job. I didn't have an address, but I thought maybe I could talk my way around that one.

What I didn't expect was how I would react in the mall. I was fine, at first, but then people started to bump into me. My heart started to pound in my chest, my chest got tight, and breathing became difficult, and then the world around me started to morph into something different.

Suddenly, I wasn't in the mall.

I was back in that room.

The torture room.

I was strapped down to the chair, naked, and they were shocking me with a cattle prod every time a scene from a gay porno played on the screen. I wasn't stupid, I knew what they were trying to do. They wanted my mind to connect homosexuality with pain. They wanted to rewire my brain. But what they didn't expect was for me to hold onto the memories of all of the pleasure I got from messing around with my boyfriend before I was trapped here.

"Homosexuality is a disease. The only way to cure you, is to remove it from your body," Ralph, one of the men who worked at the camp, barked once again before he pushed the cattle prod into my side.

I had tried to stop screaming when they did it—they seemed to enjoy the screams—but no matter how hard I tried, I couldn't keep the screams in. The pain was always horrific, no matter how many times it had happened to me. They knew where to push the prod to inflict the most pain.

EVIE RILEY

I knew the electrical burns would stay for weeks, but it wouldn't stop them from strapping me down to this chair. I did my best to try and block it all out. To block out the vile and cruel words they were spewing at me. I knew what would come next. Once they were done showing me how painful being gay was, they would take it to the next level.

Jessica.

A prostitute who got paid to sleep with the guys here in the camp.

I had never had sex with her, but she would give me oral and I would close my eyes and pretend that she was a guy. Sometimes, in the beginning, I could get hard. But recently, I couldn't even get hard anymore. That only made it go longer, because they wouldn't stop until I finally shot my load or hours went by and there was clearly no point.

I was always caught between hating the pain and hating her touching me. At first, I hated when she touched me. I preferred to be tortured over being touched. But as time went on, I would prefer her touching me over the pain. I hated it, but at least it didn't hurt. Physically, anyway.

"Stop resisting," a male voice said beside my ear.

I was suddenly on the ground with an unknown burly man on top of me. I couldn't see much, just random shoes and unrecognizable voices.

I wasn't in the torture room any longer.

I was in the mall.

My hands were pulled behind my back and I felt the cold metal of handcuffs as they were snapped tight around both wrists. I was being arrested, but I had no idea why.

"Get off of me, I didn't do anything," I said as I tried to get free. I didn't want him touching me and I didn't want my hands cuffed. I needed my hands free. I had to be able to defend myself. My heart pounded in my chest and bile crept up my throat.

"You're under arrest for destruction of property. Get up," the police officer said as he pulled my arms and I forced my body to move to stand.

I had no idea what he was talking about. I didn't destroy anything. Once I was standing, he started to walk me through the mall. It didn't take long for me to see that the place I was about to apply at, their whole storefront was destroyed. There was broken glass everywhere and, apparently, I was to blame for it. I didn't know why, though. I couldn't remember anything after my chest had become tight and I felt like I couldn't breathe.

Could I really have done that?

The officer placed me into the back of his squad car and I had no choice but to sit there as he drove me to the station. I had never been arrested before, so I had no idea what was going to happen or how it all worked. I couldn't bring myself to ask any questions, though. I stayed silent the whole short ride and once we stopped, he pulled me out and guided me into the station.

I could feel everyone's eyes on me as he guided me over to one of the two holding cells in the station. The one was empty and the other had ten guys already in it. When he guided me over to that one, my heart started to pound, I felt heat rush through my entire body, and it got hard for me to breathe again. It was in that moment that I decided to break my silence.

"Please, don't put me in that one."

I didn't care if it sounded like I was begging, I couldn't be locked in there with that many people. It was too small and too crowded. If I was going to be stuck here until morning, I couldn't do it in that cell. Thankfully, the police officer seemed to take pity on me and he brought me over to the empty cell. He gently removed my cuffs as he spoke.

"I'll be right back with some paperwork."

I couldn't contain the flinch at the

sound of the cell door being closed behind me. I went over to the farthest corner in the cell and sat down on the bench, bringing my legs up against my chest as tightly as I could.

I had been trapped in cells before, but they were to isolate and torture you in. Some were smaller. A lot smaller. One I was kept in wasn't even big enough for me to lay flat in. I normally passed out from lack of oxygen before anyone pulled me out. I didn't do well in rooms like this. I didn't do well anywhere, but I was trying. I guess I don't get a point for that.

I'm not sure how long I sat there alone before the cell door was opening and the officer was back. He had a clipboard, which I knew contained his paperwork, and a water bottle and a sandwich. He walked over to the bench and sat down just a bit away from me. He placed the water bottle and sandwich down in front of me as he spoke.

"I thought maybe you might be hungry. My name is Detective Roland Wright. Can I have your name?"

"Eli Edwards," I said, not touching the offered food or water. I knew better than that. Anything could be drugged. Anyone could want something in return for it. It was just better not to eat it, even if I hadn't eaten all week.

"Thank you. I am going to fill out this paperwork and then take you down to the courthouse. Judge Wilson will see you and let you know what he is going to expect you to do and then you can go home."

"Wait, what?" I asked confused.

I had been arrested. I didn't know

much about the law, but I did know that I should be stuck here until tomorrow and then I'd be taken in front of a judge to see if I could be granted bail, something I wouldn't be able to afford, anyway, and then, because I couldn't pay, I'd be stuck in jail.

Why was everything moving so fast?

"I saw your wrists, the scars," he said gently.

I pulled my sleeves down to make sure my wrists were covered. I hated the scars, but there was nothing I could do about them. It was from the restraints.

"You are one of the camp survivors."

"Most call us victims." I hated that word but that was what everyone called us.

A victim.

For some reason, that made me feel

worse.

"You're a survivor, Eli. You survived a level of hell that I can't even begin to understand. But you aren't a victim, because you got out. You are here and fighting for your life back." He offered me a warm smile. His words were kind, but I wasn't sure if that was what I was doing, fighting. It felt more like I was drowning.

"And to answer your question, what happened to you today was called a flashback. You didn't mean to cause damage. We know that. You didn't know what you were doing while you were in that fugue state. I've called Judge Wilson and the store owner and explained your situation. Judge Wilson is holding an emergency hearing where he will tell you what you need to do to get the arrest off your record. What you went through, Eli, you are going to struggle and you don't deserve to be punished for something that is out of your control."

I was trying my best not to let his words affect me, but it was a losing battle. All I could do was focus on not allowing the tears that built up in my eyes to escape. I couldn't remember the last time someone was this nice to me.

He didn't talk down to me like I was a little kid, like the doctors or nurses did in the hospital. He talked to me like I was an adult.

An adult who was hurting.

He didn't have to be kind. He wasn't obligated to be. He could have easily tossed me away in the other cell and left me there until morning, but he didn't. He was genuinely being nice and I couldn't for the life of me remember what that felt like.

"Thank you."

He deserved to have so much more than that, but that was all I could come up with to say. Thankfully, he understood exactly what words I couldn't get out.

We spent the next hour going over the paperwork and I offered what information I could about the outburst. I didn't really remember any of it, but I told him what I did remember and that seemed to be good enough.

Once the paperwork was done, he took me out of the cell, thankfully, without the cuffs, and took me out to his car. He helped me climb into the front seat, another surprise considering I was supposed to be in the back seat.

We drove in comfortable silence the

short distance to the courthouse. Once there, I followed Officer Wright as he went through the procedures to get in and get me taken down to the proper courtroom where Judge Wilson would be. It all happened pretty quickly and he even stayed with me as I was in the courtroom.

I stood as Judge Wilson walked into the room and made his way over to his bench. I really didn't know what to do at this point. I had only ever seen a few television shows and not really any of them had any courtroom scenes.

It wasn't often I was allowed to watch television growing up and then it wasn't allowed in the camp. There were a lot of entertainment things I missed out on.

Officer Wright instructed me to sit down as Judge Wilson spoke. I complied without question.

"Eli Edwards, it has been brought to my court that you caused damage to a store front at the mall. I have spoken with the store owner and there is ten thousand dollars in damage. Now, Detective Wright has informed me that you are one of the conversion camp survivors and that you were not aware of your actions at the time. You were apparently in the midst of a flashback and had no cognitive awareness of your actions. I have explained that to the store owners and they have agreed to drop the charges if you pay for the damages. They are going to give you two years to pay for it. If it is not paid by the end of two years, they will be well within their rights to file charges against you. Any questions?"

"No, Sir."

I couldn't believe this was happening. I wasn't going to be charged. I had no idea how I was going to ever be able to pay them back, but that was something for me to figure out another day. It didn't have to be today's issue.

"That is for the store owners. For me, for this court, I am also ordering you to have a mental health evaluation with a court ordered psychiatrist named Dr. Bailey. She will evaluate your mental state and provide you with any help you may need to prevent a situation like this from happening again. The first time is acceptable and understandable. However, you now know about this issue and you are expected to have it handled. Do you understand, Mr. Edwards?"

"Yes, Sir."

I had no idea what was wrong with me or why it was happening, but I could understand that I was only going to get this pass once. I didn't know how I felt about seeing a shrink, but if it was a requirement for me not to go to jail, I would be happy to do it.

I had no idea what this shrink would want from me or tell me was wrong with me, but maybe it would help. It wasn't just me I had to be worried about and take care of. If I was able to be better, then that was an avenue I needed to explore.

I just hoped this Dr. Bailey didn't decide to tell me I'm broken for good.

CHAPTER TWO

Alex

IT WAS ALL still a shock to me that this was my new reality. If you had told me four months ago that I would be sitting here seeing patient after patient, listening to their horror stories of their time in a conversion camp, I would have called you insane. And I hate that word. Yet, here I was, after three months since the camp was brought into the light, listening to an endless number of teenage boys tell me the horror and trauma they had endured. I still couldn't believe it.

I knew as a professional, as a psychiatrist, I should have accepted it by now. I should have been able to wrap my mind around it and move forward. Yet, I still found myself shocked by it all.

I could still perfectly remember when the call came in. It was three months ago and I was sitting down about to eat dinner when my phone rang. I didn't recognize the number, but that never stopped me before from answering it. I had many patients, most of which were older, but I never wanted to miss a call from them. Given my work, I couldn't take the risk that it wasn't something important. If I could help my patient, I didn't care what hour of the day or night it was. If they were on the edge and tempted to fall off, I was not going to risk missing that call. Missing that chance to pull them back from the edge and keep them going for another day.

I never expected for it to be a detective calling me to inform me of a large number of male teenage victims at the hospital. They were calling in every psychiatrist that specialized in those that are homosexual.

It wasn't what I specifically went to school for, but everyone within town knew that I was gay and would often take on clients that were gay as well. Not because I didn't like straight people, it was just easier for the gay community to relate to me with myself being gay. They knew they could openly talk to me and there would be no disgust or judgments. It helped to create a safe zone within my office and when a patient felt safe to openly talk about anything, they talked about the harder topics, the ones that were keeping them from being fully healthy.

Detective Hollingsworth didn't inform me of exactly what was going on before I arrived at the hospital. When I arrived, it was a madhouse, that was the only way I could think to describe it. People were running all over the place, there were nurses and doctors looking more stressed than I had ever seen them. Police were all over the place going from room to room and speaking with the young males that were held within. Social workers were everywhere and there were a couple of other psychiatrists in the waiting room.

It was in that waiting room that I discovered the dark secret that was within an hour from our small town.

A conversion camp for young gay males.

A place that prided itself on curing homosexual males and turning them straight.

It was disgusting and turned my stomach at just the thought. It made sense that I had been called, that we all had been called. These young males needed help and their road to recovery was going to be a long one.

Out of the two hundred males that all were underage and potentially needed psychiatric help, I was suddenly responsible for fifty-three of them. Some were able to be relocated to their home state where they were being placed either with family or within the foster system. We all had made sure that they were going to a good home and had a psychiatrist that would work with them through all of their issues and recovery. That dropped my number down a little bit.

Out of the remaining potential clients, fifteen of them no longer needed my help. They were some of the lucky ones that were only in the camp for less than a week. They were shell shocked and scared, but they didn't have a deep trauma they needed to work through.

Twenty-three were in need of my help still, but I was able to see them once every couple of weeks. They had been held for less than six months within the camp. They were traumatized, but they were able to process what happened to them and they got out before any of the extreme conditioning started to take place. They were working their way back into society and going to school. The majority of them were placed in the foster system, but new foster homes came forward and took in multiple children from the camp.

I had agreed with some of the other psychiatrists that it would be best to keep some of the males together so they could work through the shared trauma together. They could form their own support system within the house and a great deal of the children are thriving with the added connection.

The remaining fifteen clients of mine were the hardest ones that I'd had to deal with in my entire career. They were the ones that had been kept in the camp for years, some of them as long as seven years.

Seven horrible, traumatic and torturous years.

I was trying to help them work through the trauma, but it wasn't going to be an easy, nor quick, road to recovery. I was worried about eight out of the fifteen. The ones that had been held in the camp the longest. They were also now eighteen and no longer able to be helped by the system. They were drowning and all I could do was try and bail them out in a quickly sinking boat.

A few of them had turned to drugs, living in flop houses and abandoned buildings on the outskirts of the town. A few had turned to prostitution to be able to support their drug habit or to be able to support themselves. I had asked them if they were seeking female or male Johns and they had all expressed to me that they were sleeping with males. They were unable to get aroused with a female, but being with a male also left them unaroused. For them it was easier to have sex with a male as a bottom then try and get aroused to be with a female. There were also more male clients than females in a town like this.

I hated that they felt the need to lower themselves to that level, but I also knew it went hand in hand with the trauma they had experienced. If you were held captive for years only to be tortured physically, mentally, emotionally, and sexually, you would have a very difficult time acclimating back into society. These eight patients of mine would be with me for years, all with the very real possibility that they would never recover from the trauma.

I knew the statistics.

Out of my eight patients, four would remain addicted to drugs or alcohol, two would never function in society or hold a relationship, and the last two would take their own lives just to escape the pain. They weren't good statistics nor outcomes.

I wanted to be there for them. I wanted them to heal, but I also had to keep my heart realistic. I had to protect my heart from getting attached, because the reality of the situation was, I would lose all of them one way or another and there was nothing I could do to change or stop it. Their fate had been sealed years before I ever got to them.

Walking into the hospital today had brought all of the memories back from that first night. It was no longer hectic or chaotic, but my mind could still see everything perfectly clear as if that night was playing out in front of me. I knew it would be a night I never would be able to forget.

A night a lot of us would never forget.

I think it should be that way, though. I don't think people should forget about the horrible events that happen in town. Forgetting allowed for history to repeat itself and this wasn't something that should ever be repeated.

Today, a group of volunteers were going to hold a breakfast to show their support and thanks for all of the hospital workers, social workers, and psychiatrists that had been helping the camp survivors.

I wasn't sure about attending. I didn't need to be thanked, but I also knew how important it was for me to have my own support community. Being able to talk and share my pain and worries about my patients with others that could understand where I was coming from and felt the same way.

It was important for us all to have someone in our corner. Someone that we can talk with and share a drink with. I had kept in contact with the social workers involved. I had kept in contact with the other psychiatrists. I had even kept in contact with the two private detectives that had helped to locate the camp.

I wanted to be kept informed of

anyone that needed help after the camp, whether that was one of the victims or one of the front line workers that helped them afterward. It was going to take all of us in this community to work together so we could all heal from the devastating blow. I never wanted someone to feel like they couldn't reach out. That there was no one there to speak with.

I said hello to a few of the nurses as I walked by them and made my way to the banquet hall in the hospital. It was used when fundraisers were held for the hospital and on special occasions. The second I walked through the doors, I noticed that the place was already quite packed. I could see a few people that I knew mingling with others all around the room.

The room itself was plain, but I didn't

expect any decorations up, outside of the *Thank You* banner that they had hanging over the food. There were tables all around the room for people to sit and enjoy the food and good conversation. There were various volunteers standing behind the buffet area as well as making their way around the room to collect dirty dishes.

I wasn't sure who the volunteers were, but some of them didn't seem to be all that enthused with being here. Not that I could blame them, most of them looked to be teenagers and I was confident they had a million other things they wanted to do on a Saturday afternoon.

The food looked delicious, but first I needed to use the restroom before I would make my way over there. I was almost halfway through the room when Dr. Bailey approached me. Dr. Bailey was a nice woman and one of the other psychiatrists that were helping with the camp victims. We didn't speak very often, we ran in completely different circles. She tended to focus on out of control children with wealthy parents that were sick and tired of the rebellion. That didn't mean she wasn't good at what she did, we just focused on different areas.

"Dr. Howard, I am glad you could make it today," she said and pressed her lips into a warm smile.

"I never turn down free food and conversation," I said, flashing her a smile in return. "How are you enjoying it?"

"I am very pleased, actually. My

patient group has been planning this and are all here volunteering today."

That surprised me. I wasn't aware that patients were putting this event together. I could understand where she was coming from, it was good for a patient, especially one that experienced trauma, to have an outlet. Something positive to focus on. But I also understood that if the outlet was too big, it put more pressure on them and that could cause them to break. There was a fine line that needed to be walked. You had to make sure they were doing something other than thinking about what happened to them, but you also had to make sure they weren't putting unnecessary pressure on themselves as well.

"That's wonderful that they are giving

back. It all looks amazing. I just hope they are doing well with it all."

It was a difficult line that you had to walk as a psychiatrist when dealing with other psychiatrists. You couldn't overstep by informing them that you didn't agree with how they were working with their patients, but you also couldn't turn a blind eye to it, either. Every psychiatrist had an opinion. It was why we could debate for days without getting tired. It became a problem when another psychiatrist felt that you were trying to overstep with their patients. It was a minefield, but if you wanted to have connections within this world you had to learn how to navigate through it.

"Aside from a few that are not morning people, they are doing well. They cooked all of the food, and got everything ready here today. They wanted to give back and show support to the community for everything they have done. Some are also from the camp here. It's an important step in their recovery."

That I wasn't too sure about.

It was one thing for them to be here if they were only in the camp for days, but anyone that had been there longer could be triggered by being in the hospital. This was the hospital every victim was taken to and if the person who had to stay here had been one of the longer captives, being back here could trigger their memories. It could trigger a PTSD panic attack if they had PTSD. It wasn't a position I would put any of my patients in, but again, I couldn't tell her that.

"I hope they handle everything well today. I was just on my way to the restroom and then I'll come grab some food," I said with a nod in the direction of the food table. I didn't have to go to the bathroom that badly, but talking with Heather was not an easy thing to do on a good day.

"Of course. Enjoy the food and I'll come see you in a bit and we can catch up," she said with a friendly smile before she headed off to her next victim.

Dr. Heather Bailey. She was a force to be reckoned with, but she was also a force you wanted to avoid like your life depended on it. Her beliefs were a bit old school, even though she was one of the younger psychiatrists at just thirty-three. She believed that children should be able to work through anything by simply sucking it up. She had a firm belief that her patients should always remember someone else in the world has it worse than they did, therefore, what they were going through was nothing compared to others. That may have worked if your patient had a problem with jealousy or complaining because their parents refused to buy them a brand new car for their sixteenth birthday. That didn't work for the patients that experienced true trauma that they needed to work through. Hearing that somewhere in the world a child was being starved and beaten while they sat nice and safe at home, didn't help them to heal. Instead, it added guilt and self-hate into the mix. I was forever thankful that my patients had ended up with me and not with her.

Letting out a sigh, I made my way to the men's room. The second I walked in, though, I noticed that something was wrong. I had expected to either find it empty or to find a man or two using the facilities. What I did not expect to find, was a young man leaning against the wall having a full blown panic attack.

CHAPTER THREE

Eli

MY HEART WAS in my throat.

I couldn't breathe.

No matter what I did, I just couldn't breathe. I had felt like this before, but it had never been this bad. My whole body was shaking and nothing I did could calm it down.

Today, I was at the hospital. The

same hospital I spent two weeks in after being freed from the camp. I hated every second of being in it then, and now, it was even worse.

Thc smell brought me right back there.

I was suddenly in that hospital bed, wearing that itchy gown, and feeling the IV needle in my arm. I was supposed to be helping out at the *Thank You* breakfast for everyone that had been helping with the camp survivors, but I couldn't do it. I couldn't be in that room with all of those people.

People were everywhere, some in doctor's coats and others in nurses' scrubs. All of it was bringing back those painful memories of the two weeks where I was stuck in a hospital bed.

I didn't want those memories.

I couldn't handle those memories.

I ran into the closest room that I could find, it was the men's room, and sank down against the wall.

Thankfully, the room was empty. If I had been thinking clearly, I would have reached over and locked the door, but I couldn't get my mind to function. All I could do was try and breathe, but I couldn't. It felt like my head was going to explode. I couldn't stop thinking about what happened. The more I tried, the harder it got to breathe and the more my body was shaking. I could normally stop this before it reached this point, but I had no idea how to stop it at this level.

"Hey, it's okay. I need you to take a slow breath and hold it for me."

There was a man next to me, but I had no idea who he was. His voice was calm and soothing, though, and I found if I listened to it, it helped.

"That's it. Take a deep breath and hold it before slowly letting it out."

Taking a deep breath was not easy, but I managed to do it. I held it for five seconds before slowly letting it out. I kept doing it until I could finally breathe more normally. My body was still shaking and my mind was racing, but I could breathe without feeling like my heart was going to come out of my mouth.

"Are you okay, Eli?"

I looked up and finally saw the face of the man that had helped to calm me down. He had warm and kind brown eyes. They almost reminded me of a puppy, as weird as that sounded.

I always found comfort growing up

around dogs. There was just something calming and soothing about them that I was always drawn to them. I used to spend what free time I had volunteering at the animal shelter to spend time with them.

"How do you know my name?" I managed to get out.

I knew I should be thanking him, but I couldn't get over the fact that he knew my name and I had never met him before. I didn't like being around strangers or crowds. I wanted to stay by myself and hide away under the covers. I couldn't do that today, though, no matter how much I asked to be left out of this event. According to Dr. Bailey, I needed to move on and forget about what happened to me.

"It's on your name tag. My name is

Alex," he said, flashing me a warm smile.

I forgot that I had a stupid sticker with my name on it. It was just another reminder that I needed to get out of here.

Seeing how close he was to me also wasn't helping. I didn't like being touched by someone I didn't know. I barely liked being touched by people I *did* know.

I needed to get out of here.

Pushing away from the wall, I jogged out of the bathroom and didn't look back as I all but ran out of the hospital. I avoided the main streets so I wouldn't have to be around people. I really hated being around people, especially large crowds. The unknown of what they could do to me was always at the forefront of my mind and it made it extremely difficult for me to be around anyone.

The second I walked into the abandoned building that I currently lived in, I started to feel a bit better. I stayed there with eleven other guys that were all homeless. There were twelve of us in total, all spread out throughout the building. We had used tarps to section off our own areas. Everyone was homeless and most of the guys here were alcoholics or drug users. A few of them were prostitutes to support their habits. I wasn't judging them, they all had their own history that they needed to work through.

I walked into my section and gave my friend Mia a small smile.

Mia was the most amazing man I had ever met in my life. He was eighteen, like me, and he had been in the camp with me. I met him during the last six months that I was there. His biological father threw him in when he discovered that Mia was different.

In the camp everyone was to call him Michael, as Mia was a girl's name. His father felt like Mia had been possessed by some demon from his unholy mother. He was born a boy and he identified as a boy, but he wore women's clothing right down to his underwear and high heels. Most didn't understand why he did it, but to Mia, that was what felt normal.

His mother was troubled. She had some mental health issues that she didn't do anything to try and correct. She was on the younger side, only twenty-one, when she had Mia. She had been pregnant when she was nineteen with a daughter, but lost the baby when she was twenty-four weeks pregnant. Mia suspected that had a lot to do with how she was when he was a kid.

Mia was his legal name. When his mother was pregnant she wanted a daughter and even being told it was a boy wasn't enough to change her mind. She would only put Mia in girl clothes. She'd kept his hair long and it continued well into his adult life, now. He was thrown into the camp when he was seventeen and a half when his biological father came into the picture after his mother killed herself. He didn't approve of how Mia was and wanted his son to be manly.

"Hey, you okay?" Mia asked, clearly concerned. He knew that I was supposed to be at the hospital.

I could honestly say I couldn't have

done this without Mia. He was a brother to me, had been almost right from the moment we first met. He was so scared coming into the camp and that fear, that vulnerability, was what had me stepping up to protect him.

Whenever they wanted to take one of us down for treatment, I would tell them to take me. If I could save him from some of the pain and trauma, that was what I was going to do. He only had six months in that camp before he would be eighteen and could legally leave. It was too late for me, but I wanted to try and protect him from some of that pain, if I could.

When my aunt didn't show up at the hospital, Mia didn't think twice about having me come and stay with him here. No one was coming for him and he had aged out of the system so there was no foster or group home for him.

We were sharing a space here and Mia had been amazing with me. He knew something was wrong with me. He knew I wasn't okay and that I couldn't handle crowds. He never gave me shit for it. He never tried to force me to leave and go to work. He would make sure I ate, and when the nightmares got bad, he would hold me and be there for me to ride it all out. I couldn't have survived all of this without him.

"I had an attack. I couldn't be there any longer, in that place. I just... I had to get out," I said with a shaky voice as I sat down on my bed. It was just an old mattress that we had managed to find, but it was better than nothing.

"I didn't think you going back there

would be a good idea," he said as he came and joined me on my bed.

Mia knew how injured I was from my time in the camp. He had been allowed to leave the hospital after two days, but he refused to leave my bedside the whole time I was there. He had seen firsthand what my anxiety attacks were like and how I couldn't handle being there, being touched by all of these different people.

He had told me not to go today, but I thought I could handle it. I was wrong. I was never going to be able to handle being out in public.

And if I couldn't handle being in a room with people, how was I ever going to be able to get a job?

I couldn't go to school. I was too old. And even if I was allowed in, there was no way I would be able to handle the thirty people in a classroom. Without a high school diploma, I would never have a good enough paying job. And without an address, I couldn't find a job, but again I didn't know how I would ever be able to handle being around a constant flow of strangers.

I knew I was screwed for life and I had no hope for a future.

"What the hell am I going to do, Mia? I have to be able to work, somehow, but I can't handle being around people."

"Maybe you could do what I do? I know it's not glamorous or ideal, but it's cash every night and you could have regulars."

Mia was a prostitute.

He didn't have a drug or alcohol problem, but he was much like me. He didn't have a high school diploma and he was completely broke. We didn't have anything to offer anyone, but Mia knew he could offer his body to another man.

He was very popular because of how he lookcd and with how he dressed. With how easily he had jumped into it, I suspected he was doing something similar before his mother killed herself, but we'd never talked about it. He didn't like talking about anything that happened to him growing up and I respected that.

"I don't know if I could do that. I don't like being touched by strangers. The only one that it doesn't bother me with is you."

It wasn't like I hadn't considered it. But for me it wasn't that simple. I could only handle it when Mia touched me. His touch was the only one that didn't make my stomach turn. Plus, after two and a half years in that place, I didn't know what to expect when I finally did decide to be with a man again. I hadn't had sex with anyone before the camp, but I had done everything else leading up to it before I was trapped there.

What if it hurt?

What if I couldn't get aroused by someone's touch?

How was I supposed to be with someone else, when I didn't even know what my body would do?

I hadn't even touched myself since I was in the camp.

When things started to happen sexually in the conditioning, I would masturbate at night when I was in my room. I would focus on different men and I would enjoy how amazing it felt to be touched and fantasize about being with them. But after six months of the sexual therapy I couldn't seem to enjoy it anymore. No matter how hard I tried to picture different men, different fantasies, I couldn't get hard. I couldn't find pleasure in it.

If I couldn't get pleasure out of my own hand, how was I ever going to find pleasure with another man?

"I know, but you might find it different if you were getting paid for it. Some of the other guys that were in the camp with us have started to turn tricks and they all hated being touched, but they feel empowered doing it. They are getting money from it and they are in control. I'm not saying for you to do it. I'm not pressuring you. You know I never would. It's your body and I want you to do whatever you want with it. I just also know that we both want a place together and we haven't been able to find real, tolerable work. You haven't found a place where you could work that doesn't put you around people all day or night long. Working the street would let you have only one person around you at a time and even if you just did three a night, in a couple of months we could have enough money for first and last month's rent on an apartment."

He wasn't wrong.

I wished he was, but he wasn't. And I knew he wasn't pressuring me. He completely respected the fact that I couldn't handle being touched. He would never put me in a position where I felt pressured or like I had to do something.

Just like I knew he would continue to

turn tricks and save up everything he made so we could get a place together. He would do it all with me not working because we were brothers and he loved me.

I loved him for it, but I also couldn't put all of that stress on his shoulders. He didn't deserve to be the one to carry us both. He had his own demons he had to work through and he was still helping me with mine. He was taking care of us now, when before it was me. I didn't know if I could handle being with someone, but I owed it to him to find out. I owed it to our future to find out.

"Okay, I'll try. You're right, it would make it possible for us to have our own place sooner. We deserve to have a home."

And that was exactly it.

HIDDEN

We deserved to have a safe place to call home.

We deserved to have our own bedrooms with clothes and furniture, with food in the fridge.

We deserved to have a normal life, a life that most people take advantage of having.

We had been through hell and we survived, we deserved to have something good in our lives. If this was how it had to be, then okay, I would do it. I just hoped that I could handle it, because if not, I seriously had no idea what we were going to do.

CHAPTER FOUR

Alex

THIS WAS POTENTIALLY crossing the line.

I knew that.

Just like I knew I shouldn't be doing this. That I should be turning around and minding my own business, but I couldn't help it. I couldn't get his eyes out of my head.

His beautiful mismatched eyes. I had known that people could have a rare genetic mutation that turned one of their eyes a different color, but I had never seen it first hand. Seeing Eli's eyes that day in the bathroom had haunted me all week. I told myself to forget about the blue and green eyes that were filled with fear, but I couldn't.

It wasn't my business.

He wasn't my business.

He was Heather's patient and not my own. I had no right to overstep, not even for a second, but I couldn't get over them. Every time I closed my eyes, they were there, looking back at me. Sometimes, begging me to make it better, and other times filled with heat. He was a victim of the camp, meaning he was gay, and I couldn't help but wonder what his eyes would look like if they hadn't experienced what he did in that camp. If he had been free to be a homosexual young man in the world.

Would they still be filled with fear and mistrust or would they be filled with life and arousal at the sight of a man?

I was a sucker for pretty eyes. It had gotten me in trouble on numerous occasions and yet, here I was, about to potentially do something offensive to a psychiatrist who could crush me if she wanted to. All because of those mismatched eyes.

It was more than the flicker of attraction that I felt for the young man. He was obviously in pain, more pain than his psychiatrist was helping him deal with. He was one of the ones that I had been worried about when Heather said her group had put the event on. It sounded great on paper, but in practice it was a terrible idea for those victims that were held captive longer.

I had no idea what Eli's story was. The only reason I knew his first name was because of his name tag stuck to his shirt. He seemed to be at least seventeen or eighteen. He was old enough to grow a five o'clock shadow and his voice was deep and rich. He was thin, though, and I didn't think it was from drugs. His eyes weren't sunken in like most who were drug users. I was sure he was thin from lack of eating.

That could be from any number of things from lack of money for food, to having no desire to eat. It wasn't uncommon for victims to have a low to zero appetite after they experienced a trauma. I wasn't a betting man, but I would be willing to bet my paycheck that Eli had been one of the victims held longer at the camp. He wasn't one that had only been there for six months. He was haunted and his haunted look screamed *years*.

I wasn't going into this meeting with the belief that Heather was incompetent or didn't care. I knew from experience that some patients hid issues better than others. They could appear perfectly fine on the outside, but internally they were a complete wreck. And you would never know until they finally exploded.

I wanted to make sure that Heather was aware of what happened the day of the event and that she was keeping an eye on Eli. These children had been through enough. They didn't need to be forgotten about once again. It was all about how I approached the subject that mattered and would dictate how Heather reacted to me.

Letting out a sigh, I strolled into her office and was not surprised to see her sitting at her desk, typing away. She looked up and gave me a friendly professional smile, but I could see the hint of annoyance in her eyes at being interrupted and without any warning.

"Dr. Howard, this is a surprise. What can I do for you?"

"I am sorry for the unexpected visit, Dr. Bailey, but I wanted to chat with you for a moment regarding one of your patients. Eli."

"Of course," Heather said as she held her hand out in the direction of the empty chair across from her desk, indicating I should take a seat. "What about Eli?"

"I just wanted to make sure you were aware of what happened at the *Thank You* celebration. I went into the restroom just after speaking with you and Eli was in the bathroom. He was in the middle of an anxiety attack. I was able to get him to calm down, but he left right after that. I know he is one of your patients, so I just wanted to make sure you were aware of it." I flashed her a warm smile.

"Yes, Eli has been a troublesome patient of mine. He came to me after he was arrested for making a scene in the mall. He had a flashback and destroyed some property. The judge ordered him to speak with me. He's only been my patient for approximately a month now."

"He was one of the camp victims, I'm

assuming."

The fact that he had a flashback and destroyed property told me that he had PTSD. Surely, Heather would have seen that as well. She had to know that being back in the hospital so soon after the camp would be a terrible idea for Eli.

So why did she bring him there?

"He was there from fifteen until just shy of eighteen. He was there for close to two and a half years. He turned eighteen a month ago."

Two and a half years.

Shit.

That was a long time. He was older than some of the victims that had been in the camp. I had learned from my patients that those who came into the camp at an older age weren't as brainwashed as the younger ones. They still had trauma and torture they had to recover from, but at least their minds understood that what had been done to them was wrong.

Some of the young males that I was helping who were between twelve and fourteen were struggling a great deal with the brainwashing that was conditioned into them. They were struggling with understanding that being gay was not a disease or something that needed to be fixed in them. The self-hate was rooted deep within them and it was going to take extensive therapy for years before the conditioning was reversed.

"He have family in the area?"

"He is living with an aunt. I will take note of the anxiety attack and speak with him about it when I see him next month for our scheduled season."

"Next month? He isn't in weekly?"

That shocked me. He clearly had PTSD. He was having flashbacks and anxiety attacks. He should have been in at least once a week. If he was my patient, I would have him in three times a week to work through it. He should not be left for a month in between appointments.

"There's no need. He has behavioral issues that he needs to work through. He has his booklet that he needs to complete each month before our next session. He's eighteen. He has to work through these problems so he can be a functioning member of society. He doesn't need to be handled with kid gloves. He needs to be treated like an adult and given some tough love."

He had been eighteen for a month

and had spent two and a half years being tortured. The very last thing that poor guy needed was tough love. He needed someone that would be a support to him. Someone he could go to when he needed to talk. He needed someone to be on his side and help him work through his issues.

The fact that Heather believed that he only had behavioral issues was absurd. Of course he had a big load of behavioral issues, he had PTSD, and someone with her years of experience should have easily seen that.

"He has PTSD, you must see that. The flashbacks, the anxiety attacks, it's all connected to his two and a half years in captivity," I tried to reason, my fist clenched in my lap at her lackluster attitude toward her patient's needs.

"I haven't diagnosed him with PTSD. He doesn't show the signs, and there is nothing that he has discussed with me that would lead me to believe he went through anything that traumatic within the camp. He's my patient, Dr. Howard, and I am the one with his file and his history. I am in the position to dictate what he needs and what he has. Now, if that is all, I need to get back to my work."

She was done with me and I could clearly tell she was annoyed by me poking my nose into things. She could be annoyed all she wanted. It was ridiculous that she wasn't diagnosing Eli with PTSD. Everything was connected to his time in the camp and I didn't care if he didn't talk about anything traumatic yet, he'd experienced more than enough to give him PTSD. There was no doubt in my mind about that fact.

I simply gave a nod and thanked her for her time as I headed out. She wasn't going to be the support that Eli needed. I could have left it alone. I had done my job by sharing what I had experienced with Eli and now it was up to her. He wasn't my patient and it was no business of mine how she handled him and his recovery.

Now was the time that I should walk away, but I couldn't do that this time around. Eli deserved better. He didn't deserve to get thrown into the deep end and treated like he didn't matter because someone believed they didn't go through anything traumatizing enough to warrant more of their time. Two and a half years in that place, even just sitting in a room all alone, would be more than traumatizing enough for someone.

Eli deserved better, but I couldn't just take him off her hands. She would never agree to the change and I wasn't foolish enough to deny that I was attracted to him. I didn't know him, but I knew my body was attracted to him. It was all science and hormones, but I was not going to risk my career, my license, for anything or anyone.

I couldn't take him on as my patient, but that didn't mean I couldn't still help him. That I couldn't be there for him. Heather certainly held no interest in doing it, so I would.

First, I needed to find Eli so I could speak with him in a public setting. I didn't want him thinking I was stalking him at all. The PTSD would make him have a harder time with trusting people, and it could make him paranoid, as well. I didn't want him thinking I was a threat to him.

I pulled out my cell phone and called up a new friend of mine since the evening of the camp takedown. Sebastian Roth was a private detective in Alias Investigations. He was a good man and we had gotten close over the past three months. He always asked how my patients were doing and offered any help he could give, should it be needed. He was a good man who just wanted to make sure all of the victims were okay and being looked after.

He was also a man with a secret, but it was not my place to try and drag it out of him. I did make a point of letting him know that he could always talk to me, should the need arise.

"Doc," he answered, and I couldn't help but roll my eyes. This man refused to call me by my name, no matter how many times I asked him to.

"Hey, Sebastian, I was hoping you could do me a small favor."

"Gonna cost ya."

I knew he was going to say that, but I also knew he wasn't looking for a sexual favor, unfortunately. I would not say no to getting into bed with that man, but he didn't hold any interest in me in that way. I knew he had his eyes set on Detective Hollingsworth. I was okay with it, though. I always enjoyed having a friend.

"Drinks are on me. I need to find an eighteen year old named Eli. He was one of the camp victims. I just want to make sure he's okay. His psychiatrist isn't taking his case very seriously. I just want to let him know that he's got support out there."

"I can do that. We got a list of everyone that was in the camp and where they ended up. I'll make the call and see if he's where he was supposed to go. He a high risk?" Sebastian asked, referring to the ones that could potentially kill themselves.

"I don't think so. He's got PTSD, though, and I want to make sure he gets to work through it properly. He's supposed to be living with an aunt and he's got to be local to have this psychiatrist."

"I'll find him."

"Thanks, Sebastian, I really appreciate it."

"We all care about these kids. If he's slipping through the cracks, it's on us to make sure that doesn't happen. I'll call you when I have him."

"You're the best Sebastian," I said, before I hung up.

I felt better knowing that Sebastian would find Eli and I would be able to talk with him and make sure he got the help that he truly needed. I wasn't doing this for any other reason outside of being a doctor and wanting to help a man in need. It had nothing to do with those mismatched eyes and handsome face. At least, that's what I was telling myself.

CHAPTER FIVE

THIS WAS STUPID. There was no way I was going to be able to handle doing this, but I really had no idea what else I was going to do.

Mia had suggested that I try turning tricks. I knew it could be good money, he made very good money, but even at the rate he was going it was going to take us months to save up enough to get our own place. Neither one of us wanted to wait three or four months to be able to have enough money saved up to get our own place together.

Our dream of living together, of getting proper jobs and having a real life, a life that allowed us to be free to be ourselves was the only thing that got us through those last six months in the camp. We desperately wanted it and that desperation had led me here. Standing in the rough part of town where the drug dealers and other prostitutes were.

I could see Mia just down the street from me talking to someone in a car that pulled up. We had only been here ten minutes and he was already getting picked up. I knew he made five hundred a night when he was out here, but I also suspected he had a pimp because he wasn't getting to keep it all. He made five hundred on a good night and, normally, he only had a hundred in cash by the time he got home. I had tried to get more information out of him, but when he didn't want to talk there was no making him.

He got into the car and I knew he was off to some motel room to sleep with a complete stranger. I had no idea how he could be so cool and collected about all of this. I knew he only spent six months in the camp, but he was still only eighteen as of two weeks ago.

He started when he was seventeen. Right when I could be released from the hospital, he was out here working. Either the guys knew and didn't care, or they were that stupid. I suspected they didn't care because Mia did not look eighteen. He looked sixteen, but I suspected that was the attraction to him, as well as his unique appearance.

Fuck.

I had no idea how I was going to do this. Even just standing here I could feel the anxiety on the edge, just waiting to be pushed over. There was already a tremble to my arms and hands and I knew it would be worse the second I was alone with some stranger. Why I thought I could do this, I have no idea. But the only reason I was out here was to be able to help support our household. I had to work. It wasn't fair for it all to rest on Mia's shoulders. He didn't deserve that.

"Hey sexy, how much for an hour?"

It took me a moment to realize that

the guy was speaking to me. He was older, a good deal older, easily in his late forties, and he was not attractive, but I knew that was part of the game. It wasn't like young, good looking, rich men were looking for a prostitute to spend their night with. It was older and desperate men that needed to pay for sex.

"It's a hundred," I answered.

Mia had said to never do anything for less than a hundred, because you had to give twenty per client to the manager at the motel to look the other way and rent you the room for the night without charging you. Apparently, this wasn't all that uncommon of an occurrence. All of the prostitutes would use the same motel and they got a room for the night without having to pay for it and they would slip a twenty dollar bill to the night manager at the front every time they had a client.

It might not sound like much, but there were sixteen rooms, all of which were normally empty and used by the prostitutes. Even if each prostitute only took one guy back to the motel, the manager was still making three hundred and twenty dollars a night in his own pocket. It was very good money for him and it only surprised me even more.

How could something like selling your body for sex be so common that even the motel manager got to have a cut?

"Take me to your room," the trick in the car demanded.

I simply gave a nod and started to head off toward the motel. Now that I actually had a client, I thought I would feel a bit different. I thought the perspective of money would help to calm down my nerves and anxiety. I thought if I just focused on the money that I would be getting, it would allow me to be able to do this. But walking to the motel, walking into that room with a complete stranger, the thought of the money wasn't helping.

It was getting harder and harder to breathe the closer to the motel that we got. Then, once in the room with the door was closed, I thought I was going to explode right then and there.

How could being alone in a room with someone be so difficult?

"You're new," the man said.

"What?" I asked, trying to get my anxiety down and focus on what needed to be done.

"I haven't seen you around before. You're new. Am I your first?"

"Yeah."

Oh, he was my first.

That was also another thing that was bothering me. I'd done kissing and touching, I'd done oral, but I'd never had sex. I knew I was a bottom. I knew that it didn't appeal to me to be the one on top. The times that I was able to watch gay porn, I was always more interested in the guy on the bottom and all of the pleasure he was experiencing.

Your first time was supposed to be special. It was supposed to be with someone that you cared about and found attractive. It wasn't supposed to be like this. It wasn't supposed to be with someone that you didn't know, who was ugly and only in the same room as you because he was giving you money. This wasn't how it was supposed to be and I really didn't know what would happen.

Would it hurt?

What if I didn't like what he did?

What if he didn't stretch me and just shoved in?

What if he liked it rough?

What if I couldn't handle having sex with him?

What if I couldn't handle his hands on me?

All of these what ifs wouldn't stop flooding my mind. It was going on an endless loop and there was nothing I could do to stop them. The panic was rising and I was starting to see stars all across my field of vision.

"Get your clothes off, I want to see

what I am paying for," the man demanded, his voice gruff.

It felt like there was a hand squeezing my throat.

I couldn't breathe.

I couldn't talk.

Everything was starting to go black and I knew what was happening.

I couldn't do this.

I couldn't breathe.

I had to get out of there.

I had to get away from him.

Now!

Without saying anything, I turned and ran out of the room and down the street.

I needed to be alone.

I needed to be away from him, from anyone that could touch me.

I ended up stumbling into a side alley

before my knees gave out and I hit the pavement hard. I leaned my back against the brick wall and brought my knees up to my chest. I had to breathe, but I couldn't. Every time I tried to take a breath, it felt like the tightness in my chest was getting worse. My vision kept coming and going, fading in and out, from blurriness to complete darkness.

I had no idea how long I sat there trying to force air into my lungs before a soothing and warm voice hit my ears. A voice that I had heard before and was the only thing to have ever brought me through the darkness.

"It's okay, Eli. Focus on my voice and take a slow breath and then hold it for me."

Alex.

I had no idea how he was even here,

but at this moment I didn't care. He was here and his warm voice covered my skin and started to help make it easier for me to breathe. I listened to him and did as he instructed once again. My vision started to come into focus and I was able to see his kind and warm eyes. Those eyes helped my pounding heart to begin to slow down.

"Good job, Eli. It's okay. You're okay."

I wasn't okay.

I was never going to be okay.

I was broken.

So truly broken and there was nothing I would ever be able to do to be put back together. I was broken beyond repair and I had no idea what to do now. I couldn't even sell my body to make money for me and Mia.

I was useless, completely useless.

"Nothing is okay," I admitted in a shaky voice.

"I know it's hard. What you went through, Eli, it's unimaginable. But you will be okay. Why don't we get out of here? You can come back to my place and we can talk or we can sit in silence, if that is what you need. Just come with me."

He was inviting me back to his place, but I couldn't understand why.

Why would he want to help me?

I was some broken eighteen year old.

I was nothing.

Even my shrink told me I was too sensitive and to suck it up. She didn't think I could ever be okay either and she had already given up on me.

Why would Alex even care?

"Why do you care?" I couldn't help

but ask.

"Because you are hurting. Because you're a human being and don't deserve what happened to you. I know what you are going through, not from personal experience, but from my patients. I'm a psychiatrist and I have a good number of patients who were at the camp with you. I understand what you are going through. What it's like to battle with PTSD."

Of course he was a shrink.

Why wouldn't he be?

He was probably going to be just like Dr. Bailey and tell me to get over it. Shrinks were pointless. They didn't really want to help. At least in my experiences. The PTSD part, though, confused me. Dr. Bailey never said I had that. She dismissed what I went through as nothing. She even had access to my medical file so she knew what was done to me and yet, it was all supposed to be nothing.

"I don't have that. I'm not a soldier," I said and shook my head.

"PTSD isn't just for soldiers or first responders. It is something that people can get from abuse or trauma. What you went through is traumatic and it has left an imprint on your brain that even doctors can see on a CT Scan. It's a real injury, Eli, and it is not your fault for having it. These anxiety attacks are a symptom of them. Same as flashbacks, nightmares, mood swings, paranoia, and depression. What you are feeling is completely normal and not in any way your fault. Please, will you come back to my house? Like I said, we don't have to talk, but it will give you a safe place to be until you feel ready to go home."

I should have just said no. It was the most obvious decision to make and yet, I found myself hesitating. I don't know what it was about him, but he felt safe and that was something I wasn't used to. I was used to being scared and intimidated by everyone that I went by, male or female. I constantly waited for an attack to come. I could never trust anyone outside of Mia. I always had to know where their hands were and what they were doing. It was endless and exhausting, but that was how I had lived my life for almost three years now.

Yet for some reason, with Alex, I felt safe around him. There was already this sliver of trust even though I had absolutely no reason whatsoever to trust him.

I should be saying no, so then why was my body screaming for me to say yes?

It made no sense, but for the last almost three years I had relied on and trusted my gut, and right now, my gut was screaming at me to say yes, that I could trust Alex enough to be alone with him in a room.

I knew it wouldn't be easy. I was still going to be scared and unsure, but maybe I could work through it and feel safe even for just a little while. It was that fact that truly hit home to me.

I wanted to feel safe for more than a couple of seconds with him. I wanted to be around him so I could keep feeling safe and that desperate need was what drove me to say yes.

I just hoped I wouldn't live to regret it.

CHAPTER SIX

Alex

I KNEW BRINGING Eli back to my place was probably a bad idea. However, I wasn't his doctor and he wasn't my patient. I wasn't breaking any oaths or ethics with having him at my place.

I would never bring a patient of mine to my home, but with how Eli seemed to be around people and out in public, I thought maybe we would get further in my home with it being just us, versus at a coffee shop.

When Sebastian had called me earlier today, I'd expected him to give me an address for Eli. I didn't expect to discover that Eli's aunt had never shown up and he had been homeless for the past three months.

As if it wasn't bad enough that he had to go through two and a half years inside that camp, but the only family that he had left in this world didn't even want him. And now, at eighteen, there wasn't anything the system could do for him.

I knew professionally I should have called Heather and allowed her to handle things with Eli. The problem was, though, I couldn't bring myself to pick up the phone to make the call. She wasn't going to help him. He wasn't important enough to her.

All of my patients were important to me, but I knew there were psychiatrists that only cared about the ones that could cut a large check. Heather fit more into the latter category and, unfortunately, Eli was pro bono. She wasn't making a cent off of him, which is probably the exact reason why he was put down to once a month instead of three days a week like he desperately needed.

It'd been three days since I first met him at the hospital, and in that time, I'd seen him have two full blown anxiety attacks. He should be on medication to help him through them, to help reduce the number of attacks that he has. He should have a system of coping methods to handle the stressors and triggers to try and minimize the anxiety attacks and flashbacks. She had left him blowing in the wind with no support. I wasn't about to leave him out there as well.

The second we walked into my house, Eli's gaze darted rapidly all around the room. I knew what he was doing. He was looking for any possible threats and escape options. It was typical for someone with PTSD. They were always expecting an attack and, therefore, they needed to know how to escape should the attack happen.

His mind would be picking up all of the windows and the back door that led to my backyard. He would be noting the stairs and what windows would be upstairs. He would be factoring in how much of a drop it would be if he had to jump from a window. His mind would be doing it whether he wanted it or not. It was something he could control, but not until he had a better grasp on his PTSD. Again, something he wasn't getting from Heather.

"You can look around, if you want," I offered.

I had nothing to hide. If he needed to look around to make sure no one else was in the house or there was nothing dangerous here, I was good with that.

He started to move around a bit, but my heart stopped when Lucy came running down the stairs. I had no idea how he was going to react to her. Lucy was my beautiful golden retriever who was currently six weeks pregnant with her first litter. I had wanted to breed her just once so she could experience the joy of giving birth. I was planning on keeping one of the puppies for myself and for her, and then donating the others to a service dog foundation. They would train the puppies and match them with people who needed a PTSD service dog.

The foundation was not-for-profit and they relied on people donating the puppies for them to be able to train and pair up with those who were in need. It was a great foundation and I wanted to be able to give back.

"That's Lucy," I said, as she immediately went to Eli.

I wasn't sure how Eli would react to her, but he instantly bent down and gave her pets and love. For the first time, I saw a real smile touch Eli's face. He obviously loved dogs, which meant he would do really well with a service dog.

"Hi, Lucy. You're a sweet girl," Eli said warmly to her.

"She is very sweet and she is actually six weeks pregnant."

"Congratulations, Lucy." Eli looked up at me as he spoke again. "She's beautiful. How old is she?"

"She's two. This is going to be her only litter and I'm going to keep one of the puppies for her. Do you like dogs?"

"I love them. I used to volunteer all of my free time at the animal shelter in my hometown. I wanted to open a rescue farm for dogs and horses that were being abused."

It wasn't surprising that he had other dreams when he was younger, before the camp. What was surprising was what he wanted to do. He wanted to help animals. That indicated that he was a gentle and kind soul. It was no wonder Lucy liked him. It was also something that could still be obtainable to him. He just needed to heal a bit first before he would see that.

"That sounds like a great idea. I know there are some farms that are always going up for sale in town. That dream doesn't have to die."

"Dreams never come true," he said, his voice filled with sorrow.

"That's not true. Lots of people get to live out their dreams. All I wanted to do was help people, and that's what I'm doing. You have a lot of years left in your life, Eli, you got plenty of time to chase your dreams," I said honestly, flashing him a warm smile.

The very last thing Eli needed was to lose hope completely. He needed to understand that, yes, he was banged up right now, but he wasn't broken. He could repair the cracks and be able to live a normal life. He could have a dream. He could achieve his dream and still find a wonderful man to fall in love with and get married. He could have it all. Hope was vital to his recovery.

I could tell this conversation was making him nervous and uncomfortable so I switched it to something that would hopefully be easier on him.

"Are you hungry? How about some dinner? I haven't eaten anything since breakfast today."

I strolled into my kitchen, which was just off to the left of us. My living room and kitchen were all open concept so I could still see him clearly, but more importantly, he could still see me.

I didn't expect for him to become even more nervous and tense.

Lucy had picked up on it as well and nudged his hand with her nose.

So, I realized, food was a stressor for him.

I knew from a few of my patients that in the camp they would often drug the food, especially in the beginning when you would resist and fight against them. They would drug them to make them more compliant. It was logical that fact would give them a bit of a fear toward eating food that they didn't prepare.

"There's nothing you have to worry about. None of the food contains any drugs. But if you want, you could cook with me, that way you'll know everything that goes into it," I offered.

He needed to try and work through his stressors. I couldn't help him with everything, but I could help with getting him used to eating food again. The best way to do that would be to cook with him so he could see that nothing was going wrong with it and nothing was being tampered with.

He was unsure, that was very clear on his face and with the tension in his body. I wasn't sure he was going to say yes, but he did slowly stand up and gave me a small nod.

I was proud of him.

He was trying.

He was fighting.

He wanted to have a life.

He wanted to be better and he was fighting for it. He just couldn't fight alone. He was fighting a war without a weapon and it was Heather's job to give him those weapons. To give him what he needed to be able to handle his PTSD and she was neglecting him and her responsibility to him. It pissed me off, because here was an eighteen year old who had spent almost three years trapped in hell and he was still fighting. He hadn't turned to drugs or drinking like so many of the others that had been trapped for years. He was trying to reclaim his life and he was getting no help from people. From the one person he should be.

Lucy joined us in the kitchen as we began to start to cook. I wanted to ask him a million questions, but I knew that would be hard on him. Tonight was more about getting him comfortable being around me so we could hopefully develop a friendship.

I also needed to know what happened tonight. Something had set him off and I needed to know what it was so I could not only help him through it, but avoid the same situation until he was ready to face it.

"Can I ask you what happened tonight? What triggered you?" I asked gently.

He had no reason to confide in me. He had no reason to talk to me about anything personal and I knew that. I just hoped that he *would* talk to me. He would start to open up a bit so I could help him.

He was quiet for a few minutes, long enough for me to think he wasn't going to tell me anything. But I was relieved when he finally did start to talk.

"I haven't been able to find work with having no address. My friend who was in the camp with me, he's been working as a prostitute and he suggested that I could try it. I was with my first John in the motel room and the second he touched me I couldn't do it. I started to panic and then I ran."

My heart broke a bit at hearing that he was trying to sell his body just so he could make some money. I knew it was very difficult in town to find work without an address. If you weren't into construction, it was almost impossible to find any cash jobs. Eli was thin. He wasn't eating properly or enough. Doing something with that much manual labor would be impossible for him or for his body to handle. When some homeless people are desperate and the only thing they have to sell is their body, they start to sell it and hope they can handle the repercussions of it all.

"Was it from being alone in a room with a stranger or the touching that triggered the attack?" I asked gently.

It could be either of those options, or both. It was important for me to know, though, because I didn't want to trigger anything. I didn't want to put him into a position that could potentially be harmful toward him.

"Both. I don't do well with strangers or crowds, and I hate being touched. I thought I could handle it. I thought maybe if I blocked it all out like I used to, then I wouldn't notice. But I couldn't. And now, I really don't know what I'm going to do," he said, the stress evident in his voice.

That was what made this whole situation harder. He was eighteen, so he wasn't getting any support from the government. If he wanted to eat, if he wanted to find a place to live, he had to work. And if he couldn't handle being around crowds or being touched, his options were miniscule. Unless he found someone who would be open minded to helping him, he was going to be struggling and homeless potentially for the rest of his life. Thankfully, I knew someone that would.

"My friend, Zane, he works as a manager at a diner in town. He is looking to hire a new manager to take his place. He's got the investors that he needs to start his own resort. He's looking to get someone in as soon as possible so he can focus on his new business. I could get him to give you a shot, if you wanted," I offered.

I knew Zane would be okay with him being homeless and with having some mental health problems. Zane and his younger brother were both gay and they knew numerous other gay couples in town. Zane had been outraged at hearing about the conversion camp and had offered to help in any way that he could. He would be more than willing to give Eli the chance.

"I don't know. I've never done something like that before," Eli said, completely unsure of himself.

"It's mostly paperwork and being in the office. He would train you and show you how it all works. I can show you some breathing exercises that you can do when you feel overwhelmed or anxious. I can also give you my phone number so you could call me as well, if you ever needed to. The choice is yours, Eli, but if you wanted to give it a shot for a shift or two, I could let Zane know."

I didn't want him to feel pressured into doing it. It had to be his decision and he needed to make it without feeling like he had to pick the option that *I* wanted him to choose. It was his life. He had to decide how he wanted to live it. All I could do was give him options and the weapons he needed to fight through the trauma he'd experienced. As a friend, all I could do was be there for him and help him when I could so he could start to heal and recover from the trauma.

"I don't think I'll be any good, but I'll

try it."

I could tell he was nervous about the idea, but I could also see the desire to work. He wanted a life, a normal life, and he was fighting for it. I really hoped for his sake that working at the diner would help him. That he would be able to handle it and be able to work and make a living. Getting back into a normal routine and feeling like he accomplished something at the end of the day would do wonders for his mental health.

I just hoped he was able to handle it.

CHAPTER SEVEN

Eli

WALKING INTO A diner should not be this hard, and yet, I felt like I was walking through wet cement.

I had tossed and turned all night last night. When Alex had informed me that Zane wanted me to come down and give it a try, I couldn't believe it. I was almost instantly filled with anxiety about working around people all day. Yes, it was mostly in an office, but still, I would be around strangers coming and going from the diner. It was also a great deal of responsibility that would rest on my shoulders. I would be helping to run a business for someone, a business that had been in town for decades. If I screwed this up, I could be the reason the diner went out of business.

I still can't remember why I agreed to this, but it was a potential job. One that came with regular pay and, eventually, health benefits. I didn't think I would care about health benefits, but now it seemed like a good thing.

All I really cared about, though, was making enough money so I could get a place for me and Mia. Mia would be able to quit being a prostitute and we could both start living a normal life. Something we had talked about for six months. It's what we would plan and dream together on the bad nights. I wanted this dream to come true. I *needed* it to come true. In order for that to happen, I had to survive working in a diner. It was either that or turning to drugs to be able to handle being touched by strangers as I sold my body to them.

No.

That wasn't an option.

Doing my best to ignore the slight tremble to my body, I headed inside. The place was pretty dead, only one customer and one server, but it was still early in the morning.

Zane was easy to spot, thankfully. He was the only one not wearing an apron and he wore black jeans. Alex had said I could show up in just jeans and they would give me a uniform shirt to wear. I was glad to see that was the case.

"Hey, Eli?" Zane asked, flashing me a warm, welcoming smile.

"Yes. Hi. Zane, right?"

"That's me. It's great to meet you. Come on back and we can get started."

All I could do was nod and follow him into the back, through the kitchen and into his office. I really hoped I would be able to handle all of this. I just had to get through this first day and then things would get easier, right?

***

It had been four hours since my shift at the diner started and, so far, things had been going well. Zane had been showing me all sorts of things on the computer and what paperwork I needed to work on. I'd managed to keep my anxiety down and not have a full blown attack, so I was taking that as great progress at this point. The work wasn't too bad, either. It seemed simple enough and most of it was paperwork. It would be repetitive and that was a good thing. I liked routines and repetition, it helped to keep the anxiety at bay. If I knew what to do and what was coming next, it helped to fight back at the unknowns surrounding my life.

"All right, you seem to have a handle on things. I am going to head out, but you have my number if you need me for anything. Don't hesitate to call," Zane said, and flashed me a warm smile.

"You're... you're leaving?"

I didn't think I would be left alone

with everything on the first day. I knew he had been showing me how the system worked, and he had all of these cheat sheets for me to review, should I need them, but still. I was new, only had been working here for four hours, now.

How was I ready to be a manager?

"Yeah, don't worry, you've got this. Just keep going on the paperwork and then watch the cameras to make sure everything is going all right. Tomorrow, we will go over more of the weekly procedures that need to be done. You got this," Zane said with a confident smile, though I had no idea how he had any confidence in me at all.

To my absolute horror, he turned and headed out, leaving me here all alone. I had no idea what I was supposed to do.

What if someone had a problem?

What if a customer wanted to speak to the manager?

How was I supposed to handle all of those questions or concerns?

I just started to learn how to be a manager. I wasn't ready for anything outside of paperwork.

I could feel my chest starting to tighten from the anxiety that was building in my body. I had all of this sudden pressure on my shoulders and I had no idea how to handle it.

What if I screwed up?

What if I did something wrong and cost the diner serious money?

Why did I think this was a good idea?

I couldn't do this. I couldn't handle this type of pressure. I had no idea what to do or how to handle anything that could come up.

The panic was building at a rapid pace and I knew if I didn't calm down soon, I would be having a serious anxiety attack right here in the office. I reached into my pocket and pulled out the crumpled paper with Alex's phone number and, with my fingers trembling, I punched the digits into the phone that sat on the desk.

I wasn't sure when he gave it to me if I would ever call him, but I did find the sound of his voice soothing. He felt safe. I don't know why, but he did. I had never felt like that around someone before and I was surprised at the comfort that came from being around him. A moment later, his calm voice came through the phone, effectively starting to calm my nerves.

"Dr. Howard."

"Hey it's... um... it's me, Eli."

I wasn't even sure what I was going to say to him. All I knew is that he made me feel safe so maybe he would be able to calm me down.

"Eli, hey, how are you?" he asked warmly.

"It's... it's hard to breathe," I said, as I felt my chest constrict and my breathing hitch.

"It's okay, Eli. Can you try and do one of the breathing exercises for me?"

His calm voice was helping to soothe my nerves and anxiety. I focused on it as I worked on trying to control my breathing. Taking a slow, deep breath in, I held it for five seconds before letting it out again. I didn't know why it helped, but I did know that it did, so that was good enough for me. I had no idea how I was going to be able to handle working there. If I couldn't be left alone, I could never work there. I could never work anywhere if I had to be supervised the whole time.

"Eli, I need you to calm down. Talk to me. What has you feeling panicked?" he asked gently.

"Zane, he left me alone. What if I can't handle it? What if I can't work? How am I going to ever live?"

I was snowballing, I knew that, but I couldn't help it. If I couldn't work, I could never help Mia with getting our own place. It would always be on his shoulders and I was supposed to be the one to take care of him. It was on me to protect him and be the big brother. I had to be able to work, no matter what it took.

"Slow down, Eli, take it one step at a time. You have been at work for four hours, now, right? That's four hours more than you thought you would make. You have done remarkably well, so far, Eli. Don't focus on what ifs or worst case scenarios. Focus on what you *have* accomplished, even small things. Tell me, what have you done so far today?"

"I've, um... I've learned how to use the schedule program so I can schedule next week for everyone. I've learned how to sign into the system. I've learned how the inventory paperwork works. I've learned how to schedule shipments and when to place the order for new ones. I've learned where Zane keeps all of the cheat sheets for everything. Shipments, cleaning, inventory, passwords, everything that I need to do every day, week, and month.”

“Wow, Eli, think about everything you just said. You learned all of that today in just four hours. You have been working for four hours without any anxiety. You've done amazing.”

I hadn't thought of it like that. I didn't even think about everything that I had done so far today. All I had been able to focus on was being left alone. But I had done all of that today. I had been able to sit here with a complete stranger in the room learning how to run the diner. I had been able to do it with minimal questions or confusion. I had accomplished all of that today and I didn't even realize it. Knowing that did help me to calm down and feel a bit better. I knew some things about being a manager at the diner.

"But what do I do if someone complains or one of the workers needs me?"

"You said Zane left you cheat sheets, so if there is an issue with one of the workers, you can always read the cheat sheets or tell them that you will ask Zane and let them know. As for the customers, it's pretty rare to get a customer complaint there. It's Tuesday, so you will only have locals in. Any tourists, they come between Thursday and Sunday. Most locals or even tourists don't complain about the food there. However, if someone does, you remain polite, tell them your name and that you are a new manager. If there is a problem with their food, ask if you can get them something else. If not, remove the meal from their bill and apologize."

"Okay... I can do that. I think."

That didn't sound so bad. I could be polite and if an employee had a question, I could always ask Zane. That was simple enough. I didn't think of it like that. I had been so busy focusing on different situations, I didn't take the time to stop and think about what I *could* do. I had just assumed I wouldn't be able to handle it. I had jumped off a cliff without remembering to grab a parachute. I had instantly jumped to the worst case scenario and the panic skyrocketed from there.

"Yes, you can do this, Eli. You have done remarkably well today. It's important for you to remember your accomplishments and focus on them and not the things you believe you can't do. Part of having PTSD is your mind automatically makes you feel overwhelmed by the unknown. The best way to counteract that is by taking everything and breaking it down step by step. Focus on one step at a time and don't worry about the steps that come next."

"Okay, I can do that. Thank you for calming me down."

I could feel the anxiety still, but it was at the level that it normally was. I was always riddled with anxiety no matter what I did. At least right now, it was back down to my normal level. He had that calming effect on me and it was an effect I was hoping would last.

"Anytime, Eli. Just remember, you can do this. After everything you have survived, four more hours at the diner is a walk in the park."

He was right.

I could do this.

Working in a diner was not going to break me.

Not today at least.

CHAPTER EIGHT

Eli

I STILL COULDN'T believe I had done it. I had made it through a full eight hours at work today without a single anxiety attack or feeling like I needed to run. I had spent most of it in the back office doing paperwork and learning more about the system Zane had in place for running things. Even having Zane around for the first half wasn't as hard as I thought it would be. I suspected that Alex had informed him that I had a hard time being around crowds or being touched. He had made a point of keeping the office door open and he didn't stand directly behind me. I appreciated it greatly. Just like I appreciated how he didn't treat me like a child or with kid gloves by talking down to me or asking if I was okay a hundred times today. He treated me like a normal person learning the ropes of a new job. It felt good, though, to have gotten through the past eight hours without a single issue. I honestly didn't think I could do it, especially after yesterday's near melt down, but I did. For eight full hours, I was a functioning member of society and it felt really good.

Just before I walked into the building I was currently living in, a patrol car pulled up and Mia got out of the front seat. I was instantly confused, because if he had been arrested, he would be in the back seat or at the station. Mia simply got out and the patrol car took off.

"What was that?" I asked, as Mia headed over to me. He looked tired and I could only imagine he had been busy today. Which was confusing considering he worked nights and normally slept during the day. He should be just getting up to start getting ready for the night. If he was getting home now from last night, it meant he was out all day.

"It's nothing," Mia said, trying to blow it off.

"It's not nothing, Mia. You left last night, why are you just getting back now? Were you arrested?"

"No, I wasn't arrested. He was my last client. It's not a big deal. Seriously, drop it."

He didn't want to talk about it. I knew he didn't want to talk about it, but I was worried more was going on. There had been a couple of times when I saw a new bruise on him, but he blew it off. I was worried that someone was hurting him and now I was worried that person was a cop. Someone that could threaten to arrest him if he didn't sleep with them.

"Is he threatening you? Is that what is going on?" I pressed.

"It's nothing I can't handle. It's better than being in jail. Just drop it, okay?" he pleaded.

I hated this, but there wasn't anything I could do about it. I wasn't about to demand this mystery cop leave him alone. I was powerless here, just like he was. All I could do was keep working and making money, so we could get a place together and then he wouldn't have to do this.

"Fine, but you have to let me know if something happens."

"Deal. Now, tell me about your day," he said as he flashed me a smile and threaded his arm through mine.

"It was good, actually. I was able to do my full shift without any issues. You are looking at the new daytime manager," I answered with a small, proud smile as we headed inside.

"Shut up! Congrats, Brother. Tell me everything," Mia said with a huge smile splitting his face.

For the first time in years, I felt a

small piece of hope. Maybe we could really get our own place and have careers. Maybe I could still have a rescue farm for dogs and horses. Today, I didn't feel so helpless and I really liked that feeling. I knew tomorrow was going to be hard and every day after that. My good mood wasn't going to last forever and reality would hit me all over again. But for tonight, I was going to enjoy spending time with my brother and talking about the good day I had.

CHAPTER NINE

Alex

"HOW'S WORK GOING?" I asked as we sat down to eat.

It had been a week since Eli had started to work at the diner as their new manager. I was worried about how well he would be able to handle it, especially after his first shift, but he had flourished. He was still struggling with anxiety and I could tell he was still struggling with sleeping and eating, but he was trying. He was functioning with his PTSD, but he wasn't living. That was a whole different hurdle, one that would take a very long time to jump over.

Still, I made a point of letting him know that he was doing good. I was giving him positive reinforcements so he could start to gain some confidence in himself and start feeling good about his accomplishments. I had made a point in checking in with him. He would call me on his lunch break and we would chat for thirty minutes. He didn't have a cell phone yet, but he was hoping to get one with his first paycheck. He wanted a simple pay-as-you-go phone so he would have something in case of an emergency and so he could keep in contact with his friend, Mia.

I didn't know much about Mia. I knew Mia was actually a boy and someone that he was close with. Eli didn't talk about anything personal and I knew that was part of the conditioning from the camp. In the eyes of the camp, true men don't show emotions or talk about their feelings. That included talking about someone they cared about. I would have loved to know more about Mia. He seemed like someone that was very special and important to Eli. There was a bond that they shared and I wasn't certain if they were in a relationship or not.

A deep pain went through my heart at the thought of Eli being in a relationship. I was starting to care for him. He was a traumatized young man, but he was also so much more. There was a fighter inside of him. There was a sweet and gentle soul in him, and I couldn't help but wonder what he would be like right now if he was never thrown into that place. I wanted to know more about him. I wanted to know the man that was inside of him and not the man the world was trying to make, trying to break.

"Not bad. Zane says I'm doing really well," Eli said, flashing me a small smile.

"That's good, Eli. You're doing really good," I said warmly.

I knew he was worried and feeling like he had been failing himself and Mia, but he wasn't. He was battling with his anxiety, but he was still pushing through it so he could work and try to build something real.

"Dr. Bailey doesn't think so. She thinks I'm being too sensitive and need to get over it. She wants me to take all these different pills."

I couldn't help the eye roll. That was always Heather's M.O. If she could keep the ones that weren't making her money medicated, then she wouldn't have to see them anymore. I didn't know how the woman got on the list to help those children.

I could understand the importance of medications, of course. Sometimes we have no choice but to prescribe medications for our patient. However, PTSD and anxiety sufferers didn't always need medication to be able to manage it and sometimes those medications made it worse.

A common side effect of any

medication was suicidal thoughts, not something a good psychiatrist wanted someone to have if they had PTSD. It could also make people feel completely numb. Not just to painful emotions, but all emotions. I'd had patients that couldn't smile or laugh, feel joy, because the medication made them feel completely numb. They were just a shell walking around. That wasn't something I wanted for Eli. It was why I'd been teaching him different coping methods and breathing exercises so he could work through his anxiety and not need to rely on medications.

"I can't tell you what to do, but it's your body. She can't make you take medications if you don't want them. And if you have any questions about the types of medications she wants you to take, you can always ask me. I will give you an honest answer and make sure you are well informed of any side effects and benefits of the medication."

It was his choice on whether he wanted to try medications. I would never take that from him. But I also wanted to make sure Heather didn't lie or sugar coat any side effects or repercussions of the medications.

"I don't want to be medicated. I don't like taking pills or drugs." There was a slight fear in his voice and I suspected that it was connected to something that happened at the camp. I figured a change in subject was in order.

"Thank you for coming with us today."

I normally took Lucy out to the dog park to run around a couple times a week. I knew soon enough, as her pregnancy progressed, we wouldn't be able to come out. She wouldn't be able to run around like this once her pups got bigger and her belly grew.

I had asked if he wanted to come with us today after he was done work. I could tell he found comfort in being around Lucy. In being around dogs in general, I suspected. I wanted him to get used to being out in public and around people, but with the comfort of having Lucy around him.

We had picked up Eli once he finished his shift and had been here for twenty minutes already. He was doing really well, despite the fact that there were other people here with their dogs.

"Thanks for the invite. She's a really sweet dog," Eli said warmly.

"She is. She's going to be a great mom. We won't be able to do this much longer. She'll be too big to run around. It's good for her to get out now while she can. Afterward, do you want to come by my place and have some dinner?"

I wanted him to eat more. He got a free lunch meal at work, so I knew he was eating once a day, but I suspected that was all he was eating. He was way too thin and he needed regular food to start gaining weight and making sure his body was healthy.

A healthy body and a healthy mind went hand in hand. If he was too tired because of lack of nutrients, that wouldn't help his mind feel better. Both needed to be healed and it was a lot easier to make him physically healthy right now.

"Okay."

I flashed him a warm smile. He wasn't much of a talker. He could talk when he was in the middle or on the verge of an anxiety attack, but outside of that he was pretty tight lipped. Again, I suspected it was part of the conditioning that needed to be worked through. Some of my patients, it was like pulling teeth to get more than three words out of them. But I kept pulling, because I knew it would help them in the end.

For Eli, it was going to be questions. The more questions I asked, the more he would have to answer. I would have to balance the personal questions and the not-so-personal questions. Asking him things about his favorite food, colors, music, etc., would help to open him up and get him used to having small talk.

While throwing in more personal questions about his life before and during the camp.

There was a trust that still needed to be built between us before he would feel comfortable confiding in me, but it was a trust I was determined to have with him, to earn. He was special and I wanted more than anything to see him smile and hear his laugh. I was allowing myself to care about him, and I knew I shouldn't be, but I couldn't help it. He was so special and I wanted to make sure he knew it.

158

CHAPTER TEN

Alex

IT WAS JUST after nine o'clock at night when I headed out of my bathroom and back into the living room. After the dog park, we had come back to my place and cooked dinner together before we sat down on the couch and started to watch some television. Lucy had stayed glued to Eli's side and I could tell she was helping him.

Lucy also loved all of the added attention and affection. She was a true suck and that was only going to get worse as she got further along in her pregnancy.

I was glad that Eli was taking comfort from Lucy, though. I could see how much having her around was helping him. He would really do well with a service dog, but in order for that to happen, he needed a place to live first.

That was something I was looking into for him. I knew he needed a two bedroom apartment, because he wasn't going to go anywhere without Mia. They were dependent on each other. I knew that much by how he talked about him. It was very little, but I could pick up the co-dependency between them. That could be an issue later on, but right now it was a good thing. Eli was working on bettering himself and was still able to hold on to his sanity because he had Mia in his life. Co-dependency was okay if it was in a healthy way and, so far, right now, it was.

Walking into my living room, I suspected that Eli would be sitting watching tv or he would have snuck out while I was in the shower. What I didn't expect was to find him curled up asleep on the couch with Lucy. The sight warmed my heart and I couldn't stop myself from going over to him.

He looked so peaceful when he was asleep. I hadn't seen him look this peaceful before. With how relaxed his face was, I couldn't help but notice how beautiful he looked. He was a beautiful man, even with the forever five o'clock shadow he had. He had soft features that could only be described as man pretty. His skin was smooth and flawless and it was taking every ounce of strength that I had to not reach out and run my hand over his cheek. I knew he would wake up if I did, in fact, touch him and that was the last thing I wanted.

I knew he was living in an abandoned building and I hated that he wasn't sleeping in a proper bed where he could be safe. There was nothing stopping anyone from attacking him while he was asleep and vulnerable. I wanted him to have his own place where he could lock the door and I knew he would be safe.

I should be waking him up and bringing him back to his temporary home, but the last thing I wanted to do was take him anywhere. I wanted him to feel comfortable enough to fall asleep around me. I wanted him to feel comfortable enough to come to me if he needed help or if he just needed somewhere to feel safe and sleep. I wasn't sure he had trusted me at all on any level, but he clearly did, otherwise, he wouldn't have fallen asleep in my home.

It warmed my heart to know that he did, in fact, trust me enough to fall asleep around me. Apparently, we were closer than I thought and that made me feel really good.

I grabbed a book and went over and sat down in my chair. I would go to bed shortly, but I wanted to still be out here with him in case he needed me. The last thing I wanted was for him to wake up confused and scared.

It was nearing midnight, and I was just about to go to bed, when Eli started to moan and move around. I placed my book down on the coffee table and waited to see if he was going to wake up or if he was starting to have a nightmare. My question was answered when he started to repeat the word *no* over and over again.

I got up just as Lucy lifted her head and barked a couple of times before she nudged at his face. I held off for a moment to see if that would be enough to wake Eli up. To my surprise, it was enough to snap Eli out of his nightmare. He shot up and I was quick to move so he wouldn't get up and run. I wasn't sure how well he would handle being in my apartment or if he would even remember where he was.

"You're okay, Eli," I said gently as his scared eyes scanned the room.

"Alex?" he said, slightly confused and disoriented.

"It's okay, you're at my apartment. You fell asleep. Take a minute and take a couple breaths."

I could see the slight tremble to his body and knew he was still fighting off the sleep and nightmare from his body and mind. Nightmares were common with trauma victims and I knew he would be okay in a few moments. He just needed a minute to re-orientate himself.

After a moment, he appeared to be a bit calmer and his eyes held more focus to them compared to when he first startled awake.

"Sorry," he said, after he'd calmed down a bit.

"You don't have anything to be sorry about. Nightmares are common with trauma. Do you want to talk about it? I know it's hard to talk about, but talking is the only way to make them go away. Nightmares associated with trauma won't go away on their own. You have to work through the trauma the nightmare brought forth in order to stop having that nightmare."

It wasn't simple and I knew it was a big ask, but I wanted to give him the chance to talk, should he want to. He was quiet for a moment, and for a second, I thought he wasn't going to say anything. I could see the internal debate all over his face. Part of him wanted to talk about it, but there was that other part that was screaming at him not to. It was common and I knew I couldn't push. Pushing could result in him breaking and that was the last thing I wanted to happen.

"They took Mia," he said softly.

"Who took him?" I asked gently as Lucy curled up into Eli's lap to try and comfort him.

"The Stormtroopers. That's what we all used to call the workers at the camp. It helped the younger kids to not be so scared all the time. The camp leader was Vadar and everyone else was Stormtroopers. We used to dream about the day Jedis would storm the camp and free all of us. It's stupid, I know."

"No, it's not," I said, cutting him off before he continued. "Everyone being held captive at the camp were all under the age of eighteen. You were all kids and one of the best things that kids have is their imagination. The ability to make an experience less terrifying by using their imagination. You all called them Stormtroopers and Vadar because it made them less intimidating and scary. Dreaming about being rescued and getting justice, that's not stupid at all. When you are in that type of a situation, the only thing that matters is surviving, and you do that however you need to."

I wasn't going to allow him to think anything about himself was stupid. He was a kid trying to survive hell, and if it helped to pretend like they were in a Star Wars reality, then so be it. He'd only had to survive until he was eighteen and it didn't matter how he did it, just as long as he did.

"They took Mia. Was Mia in the camp with you?"

I wasn't certain if Mia had been in the camp in real life or if that was a fear that Eli had and it manifested in his nightmare.

"Yeah. My last six months there he was brought in. He was seventeen and his father had come to be in his life after his mother killed herself. She had a lot of problems. She lost a baby girl when she was thirty weeks pregnant and it messed her up real bad. She didn't care that Mia was a guy, she called him Mia and would dress him up as a girl. She did that until she killed herself. When his father got him, he was disgusted by him wearing women's clothing and being gay. He threw him into the camp and never looked back."

Wow.

I'd had patients before that had lost a child, but I had never had a patient that had lost a baby react so drastically to their next child. There was clearly a mental health condition that was left undiagnosed and, unfortunately, Mia paid a price for that. I had so many questions about him, but it wasn't my place to ask. At least, not right now.

"Unfortunately, parents can not only make their child, they can break them. You and him became close."

"He's my brother. I never got close to anyone else in the camp, I knew better. The ones who didn't conform were either kept locked away isolated, or they disappeared. The ones who did conform were never the same again. It got too hard watching the people I knew disappear completely and all that was left was this shell. For a long time they kept me in a room alone, but then they put Mia in with me. I don't know why, other than maybe they thought I wouldn't be attracted to him. They tended to leave us alone in our own rooms so we couldn't do anything sexual and ruin our treatment. He was scared and, I don't know, I wanted to protect him. So I did. Whenever they came for one of us, I always made sure they grabbed me over him. It worked, for the most part, but there were times when they would grab him. I hated when they did it. I would have rather been hurt then left there, helpless, in that room."

"You became his big brother. It's natural for you to wish the pain onto yourself to save him. You saw a scared young man and you wanted to protect him from what you knew was coming. And maybe that had to do with him being so different. You had said so yourself, you couldn't keep seeing these young men being turned into a shell. Mia would be drastically different from any of the other boys there. It would make sense that you would want to protect that uniqueness. That you would want to make sure he didn't end up destroyed like the others."

Mia would have been a huge red flag to the camp runners. They would have gone harder on him because they had less time and, to them, he was on the extreme end of the spectrum. A male that was not only named with a female name, but dressed in women's clothing, that would be a huge issue to them. If homosexuality were a disease, Mia would be considered patient zero, someone that could infect hundreds of others just by looking at them. There was a good chance that Mia would never have left that camp alive.

"They still took him. I still failed him," Eli said as tears started to build up in his eyes.

"No, Eli, you didn't fail him. You tried your best to protect him from everything that was done to him in the camp. He's alive because of you. He's able to still be himself because of you. You protected him, even if that meant you would be hurt worse. You sacrificed yourself just to save him. The very last thing you did was fail him, Sweetheart."

I was not going to allow Eli to believe that he had failed Mia in any way, shape, or form. He had risked everything to keep his friend safe. To protect what made him special. He was tortured and potentially sexually assaulted more than his share just to protect him. He was a good big brother and he didn't deserve any blame for what Mia went through.

The tears that were building broke free and started to run down Eli's face. I wanted to reach out and pull him against my chest, but I wasn't certain how he would respond to that. All of my concerns went right out the window when Eli was the one moving first and placed his body against mine.

The second he touched me, I wrapped my arms around him and held him close. I moved so I was sitting on the couch and Eli instantly curled up against me as he cried the pain away. It might not feel like it to him right now, but this was a huge step. A good step to recovering. He was letting the pain out and talking about it. The only way he was going to get better would be by doing exactly this.

"It's okay. You're gonna be okay," I said as I kissed the top of his head and rubbed his back.

I continued to hold him as the tears shook his body. Eventually, they began to calm down until all that was left was a hitch to his breathing. I could feel the exhaustion hitting him. It was hitting me, too. I didn't want to push him too much, but I wasn't ready for him to not be in my arms.

"Come here, Sweetheart," I said. I moved and lay down on the couch.

Eli easily curled up against my chest

as Lucy placed her head against Eli's legs to offer what comfort she could. I ran my hand through Eli's hair as I felt his body relax and give into the exhaustion that was pulling at him. I had no idea what the morning would bring, but I closed my eyes and allowed my own body to relax with Eli safe in my arms.

CHAPTER ELEVEN

Eli

IT HAD BEEN a week since I woke up at Alex's place, in his arms. I still couldn't believe it had happened. It felt surreal, like a dream. I had never felt that warm and safe before. I felt cared for and it was all new and overwhelming, but it was also pretty amazing.

For the past week, whenever I felt

overwhelmed or the anxiety started to creep in, all I had to do was think about how it felt to be in his arms and I was able to calm down. It was like he was a drug and my body instantly responded to him.

We had seen each other a couple of times this week after that night, but at the diner or the dog park. I hadn't been back to his place since, and I was a bit worried it was because he felt awkward over the situation. I wasn't sure what he was thinking or how he felt about me. I clearly remember him calling me *Sweetheart* and, I mean, that must mean something, right? You don't just call someone Sweetheart when it doesn't mean anything. I really hoped it did, but with my luck, I was overanalyzing the situation and he just meant it in a friendly manner.

I was probably insane, but my curiosity was getting the best of me and it was that curiosity that led me to his front door completely unannounced. He made me feel safe. His hands on my body didn't bother me. They didn't make me recoil and feel disgusting. Everyone outside of Mia that touched me, it was always an instant recoil. I hated it. I wanted them far away from me. And yet, with Alex, I welcomed his touch.

I wanted it, almost craved it, even.

It was all new to me and I had no idea what it meant, but I wanted to find out. I wanted to find out if I could have a life.

A true life... with romance.

I needed to know if I would ever be able to have a boyfriend, be able to fall in love and have sex. I had to know and the only way I was going to find out would be to experience it with someone that I could trust.

I knew Alex wouldn't want to date me, not that I could blame him. He was older, a doctor, sophisticated, handsome. He wouldn't want someone like me. Someone that was broken and a complete disaster, but I was hoping that maybe he would help me out, all the same. That he would kiss me and help me rediscover the joys of being with a man.

It was crazy.

I knew that.

I was potentially putting myself in a position of not only being rejected, but worse, for him to kiss me and for me to not be able to handle it. That was my biggest fear. That even with a man that I trusted on some level, I wouldn't be able to be intimate with him. That I would never be able to have a normal and healthy relationship ever again.

The camp had taken so much from me, I didn't want that taken from me, too, because then it felt like they won. I couldn't handle it if they won in the end. That if all of their conditioning had ruined me for the rest of my life.

I wanted a relationship.

I wanted to be able to have sex with a man.

I didn't want to die a virgin all because I was too scared and traumatized to be touched.

They couldn't ruin me. No. I wouldn't allow it, not while it was within my power.

I just hoped that Alex would agree.

Gathering up all of the courage I could muster, I reached out and hit the doorbell. It felt like an eternity that I was left waiting for a response when in reality it was only seconds, but that time had my mind going over every possible scenario. Most of them revolved around Alex laughing at me and turning me down. By the time the door opened, I was a huge ball of nerves and it was a miracle I wasn't curled up into a ball fighting to breathe.

"Eli, come on in," he said, flashing me a warm smile as he stepped back.

My body moved of its own volition and I walked inside. I was instantly greeted by Lucy. Seeing her had begun the process of calming me down. I instantly bent down and began petting her, each stroke across her soft fur calming my racing heart. There was just something about her that made it so much easier to breathe. Having her around when I was with Alex was a huge help. She was a remarkable dog and I really hoped I would still be around when she went into labor.

Her puppies were going to be adorable.

I just knew it.

"Sorry for just showing up like this," I said as I straightened, Lucy still leaning against my leg with her nose nudging my hand.

"I like when you show up," Alex said, the most beautiful smile I had ever seen crossing his features. "Can I get you something to drink?"

"No, I'm good, thanks. I know it's getting late," I said, feeling slightly awkward. I had no idea how I was ever going to approach this subject. I knew I couldn't just lie and say I was in the neighborhood and thought I would stop by for a late night cup of tea. He wasn't an idiot. He was a shrink and would be able to read the lie easily enough. Just like he would be able to pick up how awkward I was being.

"I don't mind you stopping by. Come on, what's on your mind?" he asked as he placed a warm hand on the small of my back and guided me over to the couch.

I sat down and faced him, while Lucy plopped her head down on my lap and demanded more love. We were both turned toward each other and close enough that our bent knees were touching. It didn't bother me and that only gave me more hope that Alex was the right man to try being intimate with. He placed his hand on my knee and I took that as a good sign as well.

If he weren't attracted to me, would he really do these small touches?

"I wanted to ask you something, but I need you to keep an open mind," I started, running my hand over Lucy's head to stop myself from fidgeting my hands in my lap.

I used to be really good at talking, small talk was never an issue for me. Ever since the camp, though, I was not good with conversations. I was trying to get better with it. Even making a point to say hello to the workers at the diner and learning some things about them. It was baby steps, but Alex had said every step forward counted, no matter how big or small it may be. All that mattered was that I was taking those steps.

"I am always open minded. Ask me anything," he easily said.

I was hoping he was very open minded and had some form of an attraction to me and that it was not all in my head. I thought he was attracted to me. I didn't understand why, but I thought he was. I really hoped I wasn't wrong or reading too much into it all.

"I was fifteen when I was put into the camp. Before that, I had a boyfriend and my father walked in on us making out. We had been together for almost a year and had been fooling around. We never had sex, but we did everything else," I said, slightly awkwardly. I had only ever told Mia that I was still a virgin.

"That's perfectly normal teenage

behavior," Alex said with complete understanding in his voice.

What I was about to ask wasn't so normal, or maybe it was.

People always said teenagers, even at eighteen, were often sleeping with other people and having a good time. They didn't settle down with one person but played the field. Maybe asking for a "friends with benefits" situation was completely normal for an eighteen year old to do.

I hoped so.

"Ever since the camp, even during it, I haven't been able to tolerate anyone touching me. Mia is the only one that it doesn't bother me, but we're brothers so it's different. Normally, when someone touches me, I hate it. I get really anxious and I have an anxiety attack, like you saw."

"Which is a perfectly normal reaction to everything you've been through. I know we haven't talked about what happened specifically to you, but I do know from my patients what things they have experienced. Being afraid of being touched or hating the thought of it is a normal reaction to the trauma you have experienced. It is a trauma that gets worked through as you find someone that you feel comfortable and safe with to work through that trauma."

It was great that he said that, because it meant he would understand why I was asking him this. I hoped that meant he would agree to trying it with me. I had no idea who else I would ask this of, because there was no one I could ask to help me work through this. There was no one I could trust to touch me like I was about to ask him to do.

"I would like to work through it, but there's only two people that I would trust with touching me. Mia, who is obviously out... and you," I finally admitted.

I could see the confusion flash across his eyes for a moment before they were completely locked down of any emotions. This was what I was afraid of, what he would say or feel about me and my proposal. Though, technically, I hadn't actually proposed anything, yet. I was slowly working up to it and I honestly wasn't sure I would even be able to get the words out.

"I need you to be very clear here, Eli. What specifically are you asking?"

There was no judgment in his voice and I suspected he already knew what I was asking, but he wanted to hear me say it.

To confirm his suspicions.

I could walk this back. Say I wasn't asking anything, or come up with some lie to make it seem like I wasn't trying to ask him to be my first friend with benefits. But if I did that, then I would be taking a step backward, and that wasn't something I wanted to do. Going backward felt like failing, like they were winning, and that wasn't something I could handle.

"When someone touches me, guy or girl, it makes it hard to breathe. It's been like that for almost two years, now. It's gotten worse over the two years, to the point that sometimes even someone brushing against me is enough to cause my anxiety to increase. Like I said, Mia doesn't bother me but he's my brother. The only other person that I've been able to be okay with touching me is you. You can obviously say *no*, and I'll completely understand, but I was hoping you would be willing to help me with my sexual trauma." I didn't exactly answer his question.

"Help you how, though, Eli?" he askcd with complete patience to his voice.

"By being a friend with benefits," I simply said.

It all came down to that.

If he said *no*, then I would move on and, hopefully, find someone else that their touch didn't bother me to try with them. I was hoping we could still be friends, though.

At least, I thought that's what we

were.

I hoped that's what we were.

He was a shrink. He had to understand the therapeutic benefits of sexual therapy.

"First, I am not saying *no*, I want you to remember that," he started, but paused to make sure I understood what he just said.

"Okay," I said, hoping he would continue.

"If we do this, then I need two things from you. The first, I need you to trust me. Trust that I would never do something to hurt you, or push you into doing something you aren't ready for. The second, complete honesty. This can't work if you aren't one hundred percent honest with me about how you are feeling, any memories that are triggered.

You have to tell me the truth, no matter what we are doing. I need to know that anything we do, anything *I* do, is not going to make your trauma worse."

That was all completely understandable. I could understand where he was coming from and I appreciated his honesty. I was also a bit excited for the first time in years, because he didn't flat out say *no*. There were conditions, but they were very reasonable conditions. Ones I could live with and honor.

"I can do that. I promise."

He ran his hand up and down my leg as he spoke. "We're gonna go slow, one step at a time, okay?"

I simply gave a nod and he slowly closed the space between us. He leaned in and my body reacted on instinct and leaned toward him. My heart was starting to pound in my chest and, for the first time in years, it wasn't because I was scared or feeling anxious.

It was anticipation of pleasure.

Just before our lips met, though, one last thought flashed through my mind and it was like a cold shower had rained down on me.

"Wait," I said softly, before I slowly pulled back. "Are you okay with this? I don't want you to feel pressured or obligated to do this with me because you're a shrink and I'm screwed up. I know I'm not exactly attractive."

"Stop right there. You are the most beautiful man I have ever seen. I was attracted to you from the moment I met you. I'm not doing this out of some obligation or professional morals. I like you, and if I can help you heal from the trauma you experienced, then I'm all in, Sweetheart."

Holy shit.

He liked me.

A successful, older, handsome man actually liked me.

It made no sense why he would. I was a mess. A broken mess of an eighteen year old and yet, he somehow still found me attractive. I wasn't sure if that spoke more about me or him, but we both liked each other, and he wanted to help me work through the trauma.

I would be a fool not to let him.

I gave him a warm smile before I started to close the gap between us once again.

He moved his free hand to the side of my face, then around to the back of my neck as he leaned in. The second our lips touched, it felt like my chest exploded. A tsunami of heat spread from the center of my chest out, and didn't stop until it covered every square inch of my body.

I forgot how amazing it felt to be kissed.

It was always my favorite part.

I figured it had to do with my young age at the time, but it still gave me chills and was strong enough to turn me into a pile of melted goo.

He went slow and gentle, at first, our lips just barely touching. It felt good, but I wanted more than just a soft, tentative kiss.

When I pressed my lips against his a bit harder, that was all he needed. At the feeling of his tongue against my lips, I easily opened my mouth and granted him permission. I couldn't contain the soft moan that escaped as our tongues first touched.

Fuck.

I had missed this.

Not only did the kiss feel good physically, but also mentally.

I was kissing another man and I wasn't having an anxiety attack.

I was able to kiss another man without a single problem.

Him touching me didn't make my skin crawl.

It didn't make me feel gross or pain.

It just felt good.

So freaking *good*.

Part of me wanted to go further, but I also knew that I had to take this slow. I didn't know what could be triggering and

I didn't want to ruin this moment for anything. Plus, as good as this felt, I wasn't hard. I had no idea if I would ever be able to get an erection after everything I had been put through in that camp. This felt good, but it wasn't enough to get me hard and the fear of never being able to get an erection again was pushing its way to the front of my mind.

I used all of my mental strength to push the fear into the back of my mind. For the first time in almost three years, I was feeling good and I was not about to let anything ruin this moment.

We spent the next couple of hours kissing each other. We didn't go further and I was glad he didn't try and slip his hand lower. When we finally broke apart for the last time, Alex gave me a warm smile before his gaze slipped to the clock.

"It's getting late. You have an early shift tomorrow at the diner. We should get some sleep."

"Yeah, I should um... I should get going," I said as I tried to get my mind to function again.

"Or you could spend the night here. No funny business, I promise. We could just curl up and sleep."

Now that sounded a lot better than me walking home at midnight only to sleep on an old and dirty mattress on the cold and hard ground. Plus, the only time I seemed to be able to sleep without nightmares was when I am curled up with someone. They can still happen, but it's a lot less likely to happen when I'm not alone. I didn't know why, but I didn't care enough to go seek out the answer.

"That sounds really good."

"Okay, well, you can go and start getting ready. I just need to let Lucy out once more before bed and then I'll be in to join you."

I gave a nod and we both got up and headed off in different directions. He needed to handle Lucy and I needed to take a leak before getting into bed. Last time we slept on his couch and I was actually looking forward to sleeping in his arms again, curled up in an actual bed. There would at least be more room.

It was only a few minutes later when we were both in his bed. I was curled up against his chest, and he had both of his arms wrapped securely around me. Once again I felt safe and exhaustion that I wasn't feeling just a minute prior was hitting me like a ton of bricks now.

"Goodnight, Sweetheart," he said, and kissed the top of my head.

"Goodnight, Babe."

Tonight had been amazing, more so than I ever thought possible. I had no idea what tomorrow would bring, or any other day after it, but right at this moment, none of that mattered. All that mattered was that I felt safe again and it was a feeling I was never going to get tired of.

CHAPTER TWELVE

Alex

LAST NIGHT WAS truly remarkable. Not only did I get to wake up with Eli in my arms again this morning, but I was finally able to taste him. To feel his lips pressed against mine, and it was intoxicating.

I'd known I was attracted to him from practically the moment I met him. I had tried to downplay it, cover up the attraction for something else.

It was foolish.

I knew that.

I was a trained professional of the human mind. I knew what I was doing wasn't healthy and it wouldn't work long term. I just never expected that he would also share an attraction to me.

It was surprising, to say the least.

He was an eighteen year old man and he should want to explore every possible attraction he came across. He shouldn't settle down and have a relationship. Aside from that, though, he also spent two and a half years in a camp that did nothing but abuse and torture the homosexuality out of young males. I didn't know how deep the conditioning went with him. All I could do was gauge it from my current patients. However, each one was different and there was no set chart that I could use to gauge how the conditioning was affecting him.

I have patients that spent years in the camp who are very sexually active right now, with males, and trying to make up for lost time. Then, on the other side of it, I have patients who spent months in the camp and can't even look at another male without feeling a physical pain. It all just depended on how their mind handled their trauma and experience in the camp.

I was very pleased to see that Eli did not have any form of anxiety about kissing me or sleeping in bed with me last night. It was a good sign, one I was hoping would continue.

I knew we would need to take things

slow, just because he enjoyed kissing me didn't mean his mind would be able to handle anything more serious right away. We had to go slow and allow him to make the first move when he was ready to move things along. I had no problem with taking things slow and letting him have full control over the sexual aspects of our new relationship.

I was meeting Eli at his work for his lunch break, but first I wanted to try and see if I could help him with his living situation. I was going to visit one of my newer friends, Dominic O'Conner, to see about an apartment for Eli and Mia.

Dominic was newer in town. He had moved here three months ago looking for a fresh start after his son was killed. His son was only fifteen at the time of his death. I didn't know the circumstances surrounding his son's death, I just knew Dominic received a settlement, a very large one, and moved here after purchasing a five storey apartment building.

I knew Dominic was gay. His son was the result of a high school girlfriend who ended up pregnant after he slept with her one time. That single time told him he was gay and made him a father.

We'd shared a beer and a meal together numerous times over the past three months. Dominic was a good man, in pain and grieving, but a good man. He had been volunteering at the homeless shelters and soup kitchens. He had just rolled into town not long after the camp victims were discovered. He had been helping where he could for the children.

Dominic cared a great deal for

children and had been an important advocate for them. He was working on building a youth shelter that would double as a community center but also provide rooms that kids who needed a safe place could go at night to sleep instead of on the streets. He hadn't gotten it up and running yet, though. He had to get approval through the town counsel, which was taking longer because, despite everything that had happened, the town didn't want to shine any light on the issues within it.

I was trying to help him with it, because it was an amazing idea and something the children in this town needed. There was a lot of red tape we were working through, but we were both determined to make it happen.

Walking into his apartment building,

I strolled over to the right corner where Dominic's office was. He was still working as the manager and would leave at night to go to his house, but all in all he worked long, grueling hours. The second I walked in his office, he turned to see who was here with him. He had dark bags under his eyes and I knew he was having a hard time with everything still. The loss of his son was pulling him under the darkness and if he didn't begin to work through it he was going to be swallowed whole.

"Alex, what brings you by?" he asked. He didn't even try to offer a smile. He knew I would see right through it.

"I wanted to talk to you about the available two bedrooms that you have. I saw you posted it in the newspaper."

I had never asked him for something

like this before and I had no idea how well he would take it. He could be insulted that I was about to ask him if he would be willing to rent to two eighteen year olds and, hopefully, look the other way on first and last month's rent.

"Yeah, it's still available. I've had a couple of people come and look at it, but nothing firm yet. Do you know someone?"

"Yes, actually. Eli and Mia are brothers and they are both just recently eighteen. They are survivors from the conversion camp. Mia was there for roughly six months. Eli, though, he spent two and a half years in the camp."

"Fuck, the stupidity of parents never ceases to amaze me. I am assuming they have aged out of the system?"

"I am not certain about Mia, but I know Eli's aunt was allegedly supposed to pick him up, and she never showed. They were both rescued when they were seventeen and for the past almost four months roughly, they have been living in an abandoned building together. They are hoping to save up enough money to get a place together."

"Are they working?" he asked as he sat back in his chair, crossing one leg over the other knee.

"Eli has been working for a couple of weeks, now, as the new manager at the diner. He will be making just over three grand a month. Mia is working as a prostitute and I know that is not good. However, I believe he's only doing it as a way to make money without having a set address. I think, with a home, he will apply for legal jobs and make a steady paycheck."

I was asking a lot, I knew that. Eli would be able to afford the apartment off just his salary alone, but I was asking Dominic to take a risk on the two of them as a landlord. It was a lot to ask of someone and if he said no I would completely respect it and understand.

I could see him debating over the information I'd just given him. I knew he wanted to help the survivors of the conversion camp wherever he could, but this would be him taking in two of them and hoping they didn't screw him over. At least, he was thinking about it and not saying no flat out.

"I'll sign them on a month to month lease. Because of their situation and everything they have gone through, I'll void the up front first and last month's and they can move in right away and start paying me rent on the first. That will give them enough time to get the rent for next month together without stressing over it. *But,* I want you to make it very clear that it is a month to month lease and if they miss their rent payment or Mia brings Johns to the apartment, they are out. I'll give them a chance, but they only get one."

Yes!

"Thank you so much, Dom. They will both greatly appreciate it and they won't do anything to insult the offer. I promise you, they are good young men. They just need someone willing to offer the help they need to get on their feet and start to build that life."

I couldn't believe this. He was going

to rent to them. They would be able to move in right away and be free from that abandoned building. It would be a huge help to the both of them, especially Eli with his PTSD. It would allow him to have a place where he could feel safe and be able to shut the door and lock it. That was going to really help with his mental health recovery process.

"They've been through a lot, it's the least I can do." Dominic reached over and grabbed two keys before he handed them to me and continued. "Here's the keys. It's apartment number ten. They can move in tomorrow, if they want. I am assuming they won't have any furniture. I know some of the local shops have been collecting donations and a donor list for some of the camp survivors that are aging out to help them."

"I will reach out to them and see if I can secure some furniture for them. I truly appreciate this, Dom, really, I owe you huge."

"You've helped me out as well. Don't worry about it. I hope this helps them."

"It will. Thank you," I said one more time, flashing him a smile before I headed back out. I needed to speak with a lot more people now to see what I would be able to get donated for Eli and Mia. Tonight was going to be the last night they would have to sleep in that abandoned building. Tomorrow night they would be safe in their own apartment.

CHAPTER THIRTEEN

Alex

I EASILY SPOTTED Eli the second I walked into the diner. He had already had the cook make our orders for us and he was placing the plates down on the table at the booth. I flashed him a warm smile as I made my way over to him.

"Afternoon, Sweetheart," I said, before I placed a kiss on his cheek.

"Hey, Babe. How has your day been so far?" he asked as we both sat down.

"It's been productive. But first, I want to hear about your morning. Is work going okay?"

"Yeah, it's going smoothly. We had a shipment this morning and I was able to fill out all of the paperwork without needing to use the cheat sheet. Zane said I was doing really well and that the owner was happy with me," he said and flashed me a warm and proud smile.

"That's amazing to hear. I knew you could do this. How has it been mentally?"

I was still very worried about his PTSD. It was not something that he would be magically cured from. It was going to be a lifelong battle and he was going to have a lot of great days, but then he would be hit by bad ones. The times in between the good and bad days would grow and he would have less bad days over good ones. But those bad days would still exist and they could sneak up on him out of nowhere. I was going to be there for him on those bad days, no matter what.

"Some days are harder than others. I'm getting used to the routine of it. There was always a routine in the camp. I hated what we would have to go through, but having a routine helped."

"That's very common with people who have PTSD. They find having a set routine in their day to be very helpful. It's the unknowns that affects a person's mind the most and with having a set routine you reduce the number of unknowns. You are doing really good, though, Sweetheart."

"At least you think so. I got a call from the pharmacy. Dr. Bailey put in a prescription order for diazepam. She left me a voicemail telling me to take two a day and then schedule an appointment in three months to see how the medication is working."

"Do you know the dosage?"

"Fifteen milligrams, twice a day."

I winced, my anger at his psychiatrist rising once more.

"Is that high?" he asked, clearly slightly confused.

"Most start at five milligrams. Fifteen is high."

Fifteen milligrams would leave him feeling empty and numb. It was a way for Heather to get him out of her life. So she could focus on the patients with deep pockets.

"What does it do?"

I didn't want him to be on it, but I also had to respect his wishes if he thought he should be trying it. All I could do was give him all of the information and then let him decide if it was right for him or not.

"It's a drug that is used for anti-anxiety. It will help to reduce the anxiety that you feel. However, it comes with a good number of side effects, and, at that level, your body would be in for a shock until it adjusts. The most common feeling that patients experience is a complete numbness. They can't feel the anxiety, but they also can't feel anything, including happiness. Some have explained it as feeling like a zombie."

"I don't want to feel the anxiety all the time, but I don't want to feel like I'm dead, either. Do I have to be on medication, is that the only way to get better?"

"No, it's one way, but it's not the only way. Each psychiatrist is different. Some prefer to prescribe medications and some prefer to only prescribe them as a last resort. I tend to not like prescribing medications because they come with side effects and people become dependent on it."

"I know you're not my doctor, but, hypothetically, say you were, would you recommend it?"

This was a dangerous line to be walking, but I could see he was genuinely confused and uncertain about how to proceed. I couldn't tell him what to do, but I could talk to him about it as a friend who happened to have a medical background.

"Even if I was your doctor, I couldn't tell you what to do. That has to be your decision, Sweetheart. However, there are alternatives to medications. You have PTSD, even if Heather doesn't want to diagnose it. Your symptoms are a perfect match for it. PTSD comes with flashbacks, nightmares, anxiety, paranoia, irritability, depression, and insomnia. One way to fight the effects is through medication like diazepam. But there are other weapons that you could use. Like the breathing exercises, talking through nightmares and triggers. Something that has been a huge help to people with PTSD is a service dog. I am sure you have noticed how calmer you feel around Lucy."

"Things don't feel as bad around her. I didn't know if it was her or you, though," he said with a small shy smile.

"I hope it's both," I said back, flashing him a smile before I continued. "Dogs have been known to help calm the anxiety and nerves, it's why a lot of people with PTSD will have a service dog. It's something you could look into and consider when you are ready. It's completely up to you if you want to try the medication or not. But, yes, there are other things you can do as well."

"I don't want to be stuck on some medication for the rest of my life. I want to try and do it without needing it. I know I have a long way to go, but things have started to get a bit easier. The breathing exercises help, and the routine of working. I'm not getting much sleep, but that might get better once we are in our own place."

"Sleep will come, it's going to take some time. On that note, though, I do have some good news to tell you."

I was really hoping he wasn't going to be upset with me for reaching out and speaking with Dominic. I didn't think about him reacting poorly when I did it this morning, but now that I was sitting down with him and about to tell him, it hit me that he might be offended that I overstepped like this.

"What's that?"

"Keep in mind I did this out of the goodness of my heart. But I have a friend, Dominic, and he owns a five storey apartment building. He has a two bedroom available right away and he has agreed to allow you and Mia to move in. He knows that you both are camp survivors so he's waving the first and last month's rent that would normally be needed for you to move in. It's on a month to month lease and he's a little apprehensive with Mia being a prostitute, but he's willing to give you both the chance."

"Really?"

The complete joy that filled his eyes told me that I hadn't overstepped and he wasn't mad at me about it. Seeing his elation also flooded my own heart with a warmth to see the pure happiness in his eyes. I had wondered if I would ever be able to see him truly happy and it felt amazing to witness at that moment.

"Yes, you can move in tomorrow. I reached out to some of the local shops, too. They have been collecting donations over the past few months for the camp survivors that are aging out of the system and they have furniture for you. Beds, and things for your kitchen. Another friend of mine has a truck that he is letting us borrow tomorrow to pick everything up. I already have the keys for you," I said as I pulled them out and placed them down on the table between us.

He took them and looked completely shocked, as if he wasn't expecting all of this to be real.

"I can't believe this. I don't even know what to say. Thank you doesn't seem to come close to covering it. With this place, Mia can stop prostituting and get a normal job. We can both start to have a normal life. This is unbelievable."

It made me feel so good to hear that he wasn't upset with me for overstepping or helping. I just wanted him to be happy and healthy and he had been doing so good so far. Having his own place was going to improve his physical and mental health to a great extent. It was vital to his recovery and I was just pleased that he would finally have his own place. That him and Mia would be able to start their adult life just like they had dreamed.

"I'm very glad to hear that you aren't upset with me. I didn't even think about maybe overstepping until after I had done it."

"I'm delighted you did it," he said. He reached out and took my hand. "I really appreciate you doing this for me. For *us*. It means a lot."

"I'm always happy to help. Tomorrow is your day off, so I can pick you and Mia up tomorrow morning and we can get you all moved in. If you want."

"Sounds perfect. Mia is going to flip when I tell him about this." He grinned from ear to ear, his eyes alight and shining back at me.

God his smile was beautiful and I was never going to get tired of seeing it. Just one more night and then I would be able to sleep easy knowing that he was safe in his own apartment. Tomorrow, I would get them settled in and then hopefully we could close out the day by making out in his new bed.

CHAPTER FOURTEEN

Eli

I SPENT THE rest of my shift in this ridiculously happy place. I still couldn't believe that Alex had managed to get us a place to live. I figured with me working, now, that we would be able to get a place in a few months, but amazingly, we were going to be able to move into an apartment tomorrow.

We were actually going to have our own place just like we had dreamed about in the camp. We could make it our own, get our own furniture, eventually, and decorate the walls with things that we loved. Make a real and true home together.

I couldn't believe that Alex did this for me. That he had cared enough to reach out to his friend to see if he would be willing to help us. I was going to make sure that Dominic knew how appreciative we both were. I was going to make sure that both Mia and me were model tenants and didn't give him any problems. This was not going to be something that he regretted.

I quickly made my way through the abandoned building to get to our space. I tracked every movement and scanned every corner of the building as I trotted through. I picked up the drug addicts using, another prostitute currently servicing a John, and a few homeless people trying to sleep. I couldn't wait until tomorrow when we would be out of here.

We would finally be free from this place.

Free to have our own space.

Free for Mia to get a real job, one where he didn't have to sleep with strangers. We could start to put the camp behind us and finally heal for real. This was huge for us and I couldn't wait to tell him.

I headed inside our area and saw Mia getting dressed for the night. He didn't need to leave, now. He could stop doing this and start looking for a new job tomorrow.

"You will not believe what happened today," I said, pasting a huge smile on my face.

"Everyone broke out into song," he teased, and I couldn't help but roll my eyes at that.

"No. Alex..." I started, but he cut me off.

"The guy you have a major crush on but refuse to do anything about it. Got it."

"Actually, we are kind of, sort of dating," I admitted as I flopped down on my bed.

He instantly turned around, shock written all over his face. The joy I was feeling was quickly diminished as I saw the black bruise on his cheek and the two matching ones on both wrists. I was instantly on my feet and crossing the short distance between us.

"What the fuck happened to you?"

"It's nothing, don't worry about it. Tell me about you and Alex."

He was trying to avoid the subject, but I was not about to let that happen. He had been hit. He had been held down and who knows what else.

The apartment couldn't come at a better time. He was going to get out of this life and not have to worry about any of his asshole Johns. Or whatever that cop wanted with him. He would be free from all of this and he could have a stable life.

"Was it that cop? Did he hurt you?" I demanded.

"It's nothing, I'm not talking about it, so stop. Tell me about you and Alex.

That is what I want to talk about, right now."

He turned to finish getting ready and I knew he was done with this conversation. That was the thing with Mia, he could be as stubborn as a bull when he wanted to be. If he didn't want to talk about something, there was nothing anyone, even me, could do to get him to talk. He wouldn't talk about what happened until he was ready and there was nothing I could do about it. Something I hated with a deep passion, because despite us being the same age, I was his older brother and it was on me to protect him.

To take care of him.

He had been taking care of me for these past four months and now it was my turn to start taking care of him again.

"Well, technically, we're friends with benefits, right now, but I think we might be more than that. We didn't say we were dating, but it feels like more than just friends who mess around. We've only made out and then fell asleep, but I'm hoping for more."

"How did it feel? Were you able to, you know, pitch a tent?"

I had told Mia about my issue with not being able to get hard either by someone else's hand or my own. He had assured me that, eventually, it would happen. That I just needed to be patient and it would happen. I still wasn't sure, but I was hoping.

"It felt amazing. I don't have any anxiety about him touching me. I don't know why, but for some reason I trust him. And no, no tent pitching, but all we did was kiss so maybe next time."

"It'll happen. You just gotta get out of your head. Does he want more?" Mia asked as he started to try and cover up the dark bruise on his cheek.

"He said he liked me and I think he wants more. He also said we could go as slow as I needed. I like him and he seems to like me. He's sweet and understanding. He's really patient and he's been helping me with my anxiety, teaching me breathing exercises. He got me the job at the diner. He's been amazing. I never thought I would be able to be in a relationship with someone, but now I might be able to. I have hope that one day maybe I could fall in love and get married. Have a stable life with a kid or two. It feels good," I said, flashing an honest smile.

I never expected to have any hope, even after getting out of the camp. I thought I would be trapped there forever, even outside of those cement walls. I never expected to be able to have a life, a stable job, a home, a relationship. I figured I would be bouncing around from one cash paying job to the next and trying to figure out what couch to sleep on each night. I thought my future would be dark, but I was starting to learn that I could actually have a real life.

I could fall in love.

I could get married and have a family of my own one day.

Hell, maybe I could purchase a farm and open the rescue shelter that I'd always dreamed of having. Spend my days being surrounded by dogs and horses.

"Good, you should just focus on it feeling good and not overthink it all. He seems like a nice man."

"He is. He actually spoke to a friend of his today and we are the new tenants of a two bedroom apartment."

"Shut up, what?" he asked as his head snapped around to look right at me.

"We can move in tomorrow. Alex was able to reach out to some places in town and has gotten us some furniture, even real beds, to be donated. We get to have a home tomorrow, Mia."

"Oh my god!" He started to pace around. "This is insane. Where is it? What about first and last month's rent? I mean, I have half of the first month's rent, right now, but what about the rest?"

"Alex said his friend, our new landlord, is waiving it because of what we went through. It's a month to month lease so we have to make sure we follow the rules and don't miss a rent payment, but that's something we are going to easily do. This means, though, that you don't have to work tonight. Alex is going to pick us up tomorrow morning with a truck and we are going to grab the new furniture and move in. You don't have to sell your body anymore, Mia. We can make you a resume and you can find a real job."

"And all of that sounds amazing. I can't wait to see the new place and get it all set up. But I still have to work tonight."

"No, you don't. You don't need to be out there with those creeps and that cop that is clearly using you. You were only doing this so you could make money for us to save up and get a place. But now we have a place and my salary will cover the rent until you find a real job. You don't need to be out there tonight, or any other night."

I couldn't understand why he was doing this. He didn't need to be out there tonight or ever again. He should be wiping that stuff off his face and we should be curling up and planning our life together. Yet, he was still getting ready and wanted to go out there and sleep with strangers. It made no sense.

"And I will look for another job during the day. But until I find one, I have to still make money. Besides, it's empowering doing this after being locked up in that camp."

"Then go on a bunch of one-night stands from guys you pick up in a bar or something. You don't need to be doing this to yourself. You can say all you want that you enjoy it, but I've seen you after getting back at night. I've seen how exhausted you are. I've seen the sadness in your eyes. I've seen the bruises on your body. You don't enjoy doing this. Before I let it go, because I knew you wouldn't stop until we had a place to live and I was working, but we have a place, now, and I'm working. You don't need to do this to yourself any longer."

This didn't make any sense. He should be thrilled to not go back out there and yet, it seemed like he wanted nothing more. I knew he hated it. I had seen it written all over his face every single night he went out there. He would spend all day curled up in bed just sleeping the day away so he wouldn't have to see anyone. He hated this, it was made him depressed and he felt trapped.

So why the hell was he doing this?

"Life isn't that simple, Brother, you know that. I'll be back by tomorrow morning so we can get the apartment set up."

"Mia, come on, please. I know life isn't simple or black and white, but this is something you *can* control. After everything we have been through, after everything you have been through, why put yourself through this? Why put more pain in your heart and in your mind? You don't have to do this anymore. I can take care of us until you find a job. We can have a normal life. That's what we've dreamed about. It's what kept us going for those six months in the camp. This is our chance, Mia. You should be excited about it."

"I am excited about it. I can't wait to see it tomorrow and get everything set up. But I also have to be realistic and that means I need to work tonight. I'll look for more work, but until I find something, I have to do this. It's not that simple to get out of the life. I knew that going in."

"Because you have a pimp," I stated.

"I never said I did. I gotta go. Love ya," he said, and he blew me a kiss before he trotted off toward the exit of the building.

I hated this.

I hated that I had no idea when he

would be back or what would happen to him between now and then. I knew he had a pimp and I also knew he had that cop who wanted something from him and had been using him. I didn't want him out there doing that. I could already feel my anxiety rising from just thinking about it. I needed to talk to him more about quitting. Hopefully tomorrow, after we get settled in, I'd be able to get him to see that he didn't have to do that any longer and it would be best for him to quit. If there was a problem with his pimp, we could go to the police and get the guy arrested or something.

We could figure it out.

We had survived everything that was done to us in the camp. This blip wasn't going to be what broke us.

Tomorrow.

HIDDEN

Tomorrow we would figure it out and start the rest of our lives.

CHAPTER FIFTEEN

Alex

I PULLED THE truck up to the abandoned warehouse that Eli and Mia were currently living in. I was not impressed that they had been living here, but I knew they were homeless and didn't have anywhere to go. It upset me that they had to live here for the past few months.

There were so many victims from the camp that never got the help they needed. And the sad reality was, they never would, because they were eighteen, now.

The government system was flawed, because it only cared about those under eighteen. Children. As if becoming eighteen magically made you an adult. One day they were a child and the very next day they were an adult, as if there was some magical wand that made them able to handle the responsibility and stress of life instantly. It was ridiculous and, unfortunately, the life they were all living in. I hoped I would be able to help Eli and Mia get through this adjustment period and help them become functioning adults.

I was looking forward to meeting Mia.

I had no idea what to expect, really. I knew some of the basics from Eli and it was enough to intrigue me. As a psychiatrist, I couldn't help but connect Mia's childhood trauma from his mother to who he was today. He still dressed like a woman and I knew there was no undoing that. No amount of therapy would be able to change that part of his personality. Still, working as a prostitute was something that could be worked through and I would be more than happy to help him. He deserved to have a proper life, as well, and to find a real job.

I couldn't contain the smile that spread across my face as I saw Eli and Mia walk out. Eli looked amazing, as he always did, and I couldn't help but notice Mia. He was dressed in tight blue jeans, high heeled boots, and a pink t-shirt. He looked good, if you were interested in that type of man.

Eli opened the passenger door and he got in while Mia climbed into the back. They both had a very small duffle bag with them that they placed in the back seat as Eli spoke.

"Morning. Thank you for picking us up."

"It's no problem. Hi, Mia, I'm Alex," I introduced myself.

"Nice to meet you," Mia said, slightly guarded, but I didn't mind. I knew he would be a bit guarded given the situation they were in.

I could also pick up on a bit of tension between them. I wanted to ask Eli more about it, but I knew right now was not the best time for it. I would have to wait to speak with him once we were alone. I hoped we would get some time later to spend together so we could talk and hopefully have some fun together. I couldn't stop thinking about his body and how amazing he felt against mine. I wanted to feel him again. I wanted to feel more of him and I was hoping he would be interested in that as well.

***

Today had been a bit weird. The tension between the two of them had only increased as the day went on and I could tell there had been some type of argument last night between the brothers. We had spent the day getting the furniture pieces and moving them in.

I had picked us up a late lunch, or early dinner, and the conversation over the meal was awkward. Mia didn't really share much and Eli barely spoke at all. I could tell there was a deep worry that Eli was feeling toward Mia. I couldn't blame him, though, because as the day went on I could have sworn there was a bruise underneath his makeup. If Mia had been hit by a John, that would explain why Eli was so tense and worried about him.

Just fifteen minutes ago, they'd headed into Mia's bedroom and closed the door. I couldn't hear them, but based on how upset Eli was when the door did finally open and Mia immediately heading out of the apartment, I suspected they'd had another argument.

I needed to get Eli to talk to me and tell me what was going on. He couldn't keep all of this bottled up inside of him. He needed to talk it out so he would be able to deal with it. With his PTSD, he had to remember to talk about anything that bothered him. If he kept it bottled up inside of him, it would only make him worse.

"This place looks great. Thank you so much for your help," Eli said, with a small smile as he flopped down on the couch we were able to get donated.

"It was no problem at all. I am very happy to know that you will be safe in your own place from now on. It must feel nice to you," I said as I sat down.

"Yeah. Yeah, it's nice. I think it'll take some getting used to, but it feels safer."

"I almost forgot... I got you a welcome home present," I said as I stood and moved over to the bag that I had brought in.

I had wanted to get something for Eli

that would help him at night. I knew PTSD got worse at night and I wanted to give him something that would hopefully help him to sleep better. I didn't need to be a doctor to tell that he wasn't sleeping well. He always had bags under his eyes, some days worse than others. He spoke as I went back over to the couch.

"You didn't need to do that. You've already done so much for me."

"It's tradition to give a welcome home gift. Plus, I am hoping this will help you sleep better at night, Sweetheart," I said as I handed the wrapped gift over to him and sat back down.

I could tell he was not used to getting presents. A sad fact, but understanding considering everything he had been through during his childhood years. He spent so long in that conversion camp, things like receiving a gift would be completely foreign to him.

He opened it and I could tell he was slightly confused as to why I gave him a navy blue blanket.

"It's a weighted blanket. It's designed to help soothe anxiety and nightmares. I know you haven't been sleeping all that well yet, and I wanted to give you something that could help," I explained.

"How does it work?" Eli asked, slightly confused by the difference between a normal blanket and a weighted one.

"The weight of the blanket triggers the same mental faculties as a hug does in your mind. The weight helps to soothe your mind and body and can allow you to fall asleep much easier and stay asleep. It's common in treatment for people with anxiety and PTSD. I know you have a very hard time sleeping and you get nightmares often, so I thought this might help."

I hoped it would help. I hated seeing Eli so exhausted all the time. I hoped that with him being in his own secured apartment he would be able to sleep better. The blanket would help him with anxiety and, with a bit of luck, the dark bags that were constantly present on his face would slowly disappear.

"Thank you. This means a lot," Eli said, flashing me a warm smile.

I could tell he was touched by the present in more ways than one. He clearly was not used to receiving gifts and that was something I would be working on correcting over time.

"What's going on, Sweetheart?

Something has been bothering you all day," I queried. I had hoped that Eli would open up to me on his own, but I could tell tonight he needed a bit of a push.

He let out a small sigh as I placed the blanket down on the coffee table before he spoke. "Mia and me had a fight."

"I'm getting the feeling you don't tend to do that."

Eli gave a small shake of his head as he spoke. "No. Never. And I know that sounds unlikely, but we've always had each other's backs, especially in the camp. Since we've been out, it's been Mia supporting us. I protected him as best as I could in the camp, but there were still times they took him. I know he was only there a short time, but he doesn't seem to have any problems from it. He found us that place in the warehouse while I was in the hospital and the second I was out, he was already working the streets. It was like it never even happened to him."

As a psychiatrist, I knew that everyone reacted to trauma differently. Mia had already been through trauma before he arrived at the camp. I didn't know his childhood, but I could speculate that he had developed coping methods to help his mind protect itself from the mental abuse his mother instilled into him. Being in the camp for Mia was just another trauma his mind protected itself from. The problem, though, was that eventually it would all hit him. His mind would weaken and all of the trauma would come in powerful waves that could potentially destroy him.

"People handle trauma differently. They react to it differently. Mia still has the trauma, but his mind isn't allowing him to process it. It's not a healthy way to cope and, eventually, it will hit him. What was the fight about?"

"I told him about getting this place. That with me working at the diner, he wouldn't have to keep working the streets. He said he would look for work, but he wasn't going to quit prostituting until he does find work. Then I saw the bruise on his face and I got upset. He wouldn't talk about it, but I think he has a pimp. He's also been getting harassed by this cop. I haven't seen him up close, but I've seen Mia getting out of the car. I asked Mia about it, but he said to leave it alone. And then tonight, he said he had to go and work. I told him he didn't need to, but he said it wasn't that simple. He was getting dressed and I saw a small baggie fall out of his coat pocket. I think it was cocaine. Before I had the chance to really ask him about it, he was leaving."

I hated that I couldn't make this better for Eli. Unfortunately, Mia had his own trauma he was working through, or not working through, and until he was ready to accept help, there was nothing anyone could do for him. He was caught in an endless cycle of prostitution and drugs.

A great deal of prostitutes had pimps and they were often given cocaine or ecstasy to try and cope with the life. It made it very difficult to get them out of the life and often the only way was when the pimp was put behind bars. Mia had a long road to go and there was nothing I could do about it right now. However, I could help Eli from spiraling with his concern over Mia.

"I'm sorry that you guys are fighting, and I am sorry that Mia is going through this, right now. I know it's hard, but you have to try and focus on the things you *can* control. You can't control what Mia does or doesn't do. All it will do is cause you added stress and anxiety, which will make your PTSD worse. You can't let Mia drag you down with him."

"I can't just ignore him, though. He's my brother, my best friend. I won't leave him behind," Eli said with strength and conviction to his voice.

"And I am not saying that you should. All I am saying, is that you have to continue to get better so when it is time to help Mia, when Mia is ready to accept help, you'll be able to give it to him. You have to get stronger and healthier so when Mia is ready, you can be there to get him through, Sweetheart."

And I would be right there standing beside him. I was not about to let Eli go through any of this alone, and that included Mia. I knew how much Mia meant to Eli and I was not about to cause Eli pain by watching his brother drown.

Eli gave a small nod and I knew he wasn't happy about it, but he could understand my point. It wasn't going to be easy for him, but he had to let Mia find his own way and, eventually, he would be ready to ask for help.

I moved and pulled Eli into my arms and he instantly curled up against my side. I placed a soft kiss to the top of his head and held him close. I wanted to make sure he knew how much I cared about him. He had a long road to go, but at least tonight, he was safe in his own apartment and that was one hell of an accomplishment.

CHAPTER SIXTEEN

Eli

I COULDN'T CONTAIN the moan that escaped as Alex kissed his way down my bare chest. We hadn't really had much of a chance to make out since I had moved into the apartment and tonight we were going to make up for lost time.

I wanted Alex so badly, but I was still worried about not being able to get hard.

As good as Alex's mouth felt against my skin, I still wasn't hard.

"Stop thinking," Alex said. He playfully bit my hip.

"Sorry. I just..." I started, but I couldn't seem to finish the sentence.

Alex kissed his way back up my body before he leaned back on his elbow so he could look down at me.

"What they did to you was to program your mind into thinking that getting aroused by a man causes pain. However, your body will still crave the pleasure of a man's touch. All you have to do is to stop thinking. Focus on how it feels, Sweetheart. Your body will react to the pleasure, I promise."

Of course, Alex knew what was going on. This man was so attuned to my feelings and my body, it would be scary if it wasn't such a relief. He knew what was going on with me without me having to try and explain it.

I closed my eyes as Alex started to kiss his way down my body once again. Once he reached my jeans, he unbuttoned them and started to remove them. I did my best to do what he had suggested. I blocked out everything and focused on his mouth. Alex freed me of the rest of my clothing before he kissed his way up my thigh and over to my soft dick. The second his lips kissed my dick, I let out a soft moan at the slight tingle it brought.

Alex continued to kiss and lick at my soft dick before he took it into his mouth. I moaned as the heat from his mouth surrounded my dick and, for the first time in over a year, I felt myself starting to get hard.

"That's it, Sweetheart, just feel," he said. Then, he started to work my dick with his mouth.

It didn't take long at all before I was gloriously, fully hard. It felt amazing to be able to be hard again, to feel this level of pleasure. I thought I would never be able to feel like this and now that I was able to again, I never wanted it to stop.

I couldn't stop moaning as Alex took me all the way down to the base in his mouth. He gave a deep groan, sending vibrating pleasure through my balls and up my spine. I was not going to last long. It had been a very long time since I had come, and with the pleasure and heat that Alex's mouth was bringing me, I was not going to last.

"Alex," I moaned out in a small

warning.

He simply moaned his appreciation and continued to work my dick hard with his mouth. He wanted me to come in his mouth, and I was all too happy to oblige.

After a few more moments, I gave a deep moan as I came more than I had ever before in my life. My cock continued to give long pulses and Alex continued to swallow everything that I had for him. My body was trembling from the pleasure alone and when I finally finished coming, Alex moved his mouth off from my semi-hard dick and started to kiss his way up my body.

"You taste so good, Sweetheart."

"I didn't think I would ever be able to do that again," I said as I tried to catch my breath.

"I knew you could. Your body just needed to be reminded of the pleasure you can feel," Alex said between kisses along my neck.

I had just enough strength left in me to flip us so his back was on my bed and I was on top of him.

"Let's see if I still remember how to do this," I said with a sexy smirk. Then, I started to kiss my way down his body. Tonight was going to be all about exploring and reintroducing my body to the pleasure that I had loved so much before the camp.

CHAPTER SEVENTEEN

Eli

LAST NIGHT HAD been amazing.

I had been so worried that I wouldn't be able to get aroused. I hadn't been able to in a long time, not even by my own hand. But last night with Alex had shown me that I could still feel pleasure, that I could still get aroused and enjoy all aspects of sexual contact with a man.

I wasn't ready for sex yet, and Alex knew that and respected it. Something I loved about him. He was so understanding and sensitive to my emotions. He knew how far to go and when to back off even before I did. I loved that about him. Most guys would have tried to push for more, but Alex was perfectly happy to stop at any point last night. It only solidified that he was the right man to heal with.

It had been a week since Mia and me had moved into our new apartment. The past week had been great and awkward at the same time. Mia and me were still not seeing eye to eye on him continuing to prostitute, and then there was the cocaine.

I had found more small baggies of it in his bedroom. They were empty and he wasn't happy to discover that I had been in his room while he was out working the streets at night. In my defense, though, he was my little brother and it was my job to look out for him. I wanted him to have more out of this life. We were no longer trapped in that camp or trapped in that warehouse. We had a real chance at a true life and Mia wasn't grabbing it.

That was the frustrating part. We had talked about getting our own place together for almost a year and yet, now that we had the chance, he was throwing it all away over nothing.

I could already hear Alex's voice in my head telling me that it wasn't for nothing, at least not to Mia. That Mia was going through his own trauma and it wasn't fair for me to judge him for how his trauma looked. I knew people reacted differently. I guess, I just figured Mia would react more like I had. And it wasn't fair for me to be judging him, but I was just so worried about him and what he was going through.

I wanted to help, but it seemed like Mia held zero interest in accepting help right now, from anyone. Tonight, I was going to try something different. It was nearing four in the morning and I knew Mia would be back soon. I had gone to bed early so I could be awake for when Mia got back in. I was going to talk to him and let him know that I would always be there for him, that there was no judgment. Maybe if he felt like he could talk to me without a lecture or judgments, then maybe, just maybe, he would be more open with me and we could figure something out. It was a long shot, but it was all I had.

The problem was, the longer it was taking for Mia to get home, the more anxious I became. I was no longer able to sit down on the couch, opting for pacing the small living area that we had.

Mia was always home around four, and now it was well after five and he still wasn't showing up. I was getting more and more worried as the minutes ticked by and when it was almost six in the morning and Mia still wasn't here, I caved. I had been calling him and texting him, but they were all left unread and unanswered. Something was wrong and I wasn't about to stand around and hope for the best.

I hit Alex's number and I prayed he would pick up. I knew it was early, and I hated knowing that I would most likely be waking him up, but I didn't know what else to do. After four rings a very groggy Alex answered.

"Dr. Howard."

"Alex, it's me. I'm sorry to call so early," I said, feeling bad that I had clearly woken him up.

"Eli, no, it's fine. What's going on, Sweetheart?" Alex asked, sounding more awake now.

"It's Mia. He hasn't come home yet, and he hasn't answered any of my calls or read my texts. That's not like him. I think something happened to him," I said. The panic was starting to hit me now that I was saying it out loud.

"It's okay, Sweetheart. I need you to stay calm. I'm coming over and we can figure this out."

"I'm sorry."

"You have nothing to be sorry for. Do me a favor and try to calm down a bit. I'll be there in fifteen."

"Okay, I'll try."

"I'll be there soon."

I ended the call and took a shaky breath in. I had no idea how I was going to calm down, but I knew I needed to try. I made my way into the kitchen and put on some coffee. It wasn't for myself, the last thing I needed was caffeine, but I knew Alex would need some. The man loved coffee and it was the least I could do for him. I had woken him up and I would be dragging him into my drama once again.

There had been a few occasions where I doubted if it was fair to have Alex in my life. He deserved someone who was stable and not constantly filled with baggage and problems. He didn't deserve to be dragged into my issues and, once again, I was doing it to him. I was showing him that I wasn't stable and able to handle life on my own like a normal adult. I hated that I was doing this, doing it to him. He was a good man and he shouldn't have to deal with my craziness on top of the crazy he gets from his job.

Twelve minutes later, there was a knock at my door. I went over and checked to make sure it was Alex before I unlocked and opened the door. The second he walked in, he pulled me in for a hug as he spoke.

"Are you okay?"

"No. I can't stop thinking that something horrible happened to him. He's never done this. He's always home and when he isn't, he texts me to let me know what is going on." There was a tremble to my body from the anxiety and I had no idea how to be able to calm it down and stop it.

Alex pulled back and placed his hands on my forearms as he spoke. "It's going to be okay. We'll find him. I'm going to call the police and see if he's been picked up. Why don't you call the hospital and see if he was brought in?" Alex said, calmly. I had no idea how he could be so calm, but at least one of us was.

"Okay, I made coffee for you."

"Thank you, Sweetheart. It'll be okay," he said with complete strength to his voice.

A strength that I needed to hear.

I reluctantly moved back and pulled

out my cell phone to call the hospital. I was caught between hoping Mia was there and not. Because if he *was* there, that meant he was either hurt or he had potentially overdosed. However, if he wasn't there, that meant he was still out there somewhere and I might not be able to find him anytime soon. The unknown of this situation was killing me and I had no idea what I was going to do if we didn't find Mia soon.

My phone call with the hospital was a bust. They didn't have anyone under his name or by his description and I knew Mia stood out. They would have seen him if he had been there. I hung up and looked over at Alex to see him still on the phone.

I couldn't stop pacing around. My anxiety was getting worse as the seconds ticked by. I thought having Alex here would help to calm me down, but it wasn't. I needed to find Mia. That was the only thing that would make me better.

Once I did find him, we would have to have a conversation about him working the street. I couldn't go through this again. He had to stop this, if not for himself, then for me.

I made my way down the hallway and into Mia's bedroom. Maybe there was something I had missed. Maybe there was something that would lead me to figure out where he had disappeared to.

I started to search through his drawers and the more I looked, the more small empty cocaine baggies I found. I knew Mia was using, but I didn't know he was using to this amount. We had only been living here a week and I had already found some earlier in the week. I was now finding more and more of them and all of them were used. I could see the small residue powder left in them. I had easily found twenty little baggies by the time Alex joined me.

"The police don't have him. Roland will be in around nine. I'll call him then and see about getting a missing person's report filed. I'm not sure if he will be able to, though. Normally, you have to wait twenty-four hours first, and with Mia being an adult, not much can be done. He'll help to look for him, though."

"He's not at the hospital. Hasn't been seen at any point in the night. I just went through his room five days ago and I found ten baggies from cocaine. He's got twenty of them, now. He's doing a lot more than I thought he was. What if his dealer did something to him?" I asked, worried.

I didn't know much about drugs, but from the few months I spent living on the streets I knew dealers didn't take kindly to not being paid. Maybe Mia was getting in too deep and he was forced to deal or had been grabbed until he could pay off the drugs. None of this was making me feel any better and the more unknowns there were, the more worried I got.

"It's possible. I'm sorry, Sweetheart, this is the last thing you need. I'll call Sebastian, he might have an idea," Alex said, as he started to punch numbers into his phone.

I had no idea what a private detective was going to do, but I would take any help that I could get. If Alex thought he could help, then I was all for it.

"Hey, Sebastian, sorry for the early call. I got a bit of a situation," Alex started.

I couldn't hear what Sebastian was saying, but I could hear Alex's side and I could fill in the rest.

"It's Eli's brother, Mia. He's missing. He went out last night and was set to be here in the early morning, but he's a no show. He works the streets at night and he normally will answer Eli's calls or texts, but it's been radio silent." Alex was silent for a moment before he spoke again.

"Yes, he's eighteen and a camp survivor. He's also got a cocaine addiction, or what is about to be, at least. There's twenty empty cocaine baggies in his room and it's only been a week since he's lived here."

Alex went over and looked at the baggies before he spoke again. "It's a black spider logo on all of them. He's not at the hospital and he hasn't been picked up. I'm going to call Roland when he's in at nine to see what we can do." Alex gave a nod and after a moment he spoke.

"Thanks, I appreciate it. I'll keep you posted if we find anything. Thank you, Sebastian." Alex ended the call and I could see he was worried, now, as well. Whatever Sebastian had told him, I wasn't going to like it.

"What is it?" I asked.

"Sebastian said the spider logo is fairly new. It's a dealer that has been around for about three months, now. No one has seen him. He uses runners to sell his cocaine and he either makes it himself, or has someone doing it that is too afraid to reveal his identity. No one knows who he is or where he came from. Sebastian and Damien have been looking into it for the past two months because of the increase in overdoses. This stuff is pretty pure, and for users that are used to getting a lower quality product, they do too much and overdose from it. Damien suspects that it might be a camp survivor that is creating the drugs because of the timing, but they don't have anything solid."

"If it was a camp survivor, that could explain why no one is talking that has seen his face. We all went through something and for those of us that didn't break, we stuck together. We wouldn't rat on anyone that was going against the rules or tried to break out. Even if something was wrong, we always kept quiet and looked the other way. There had been a few that I had seen that would get high using different cleaners or huffing chemicals."

It wouldn't be surprising to me to discover that this new drug dealer was one of the camp survivors. We all came from different walks of life and most of us were average where intelligence was concerned. However, there were some that were above average and you could tell they knew how to work the system. It wouldn't be surprising if one of them put their skills to use to make some quick money.

"They'll keep looking into it and see if they can find Mia. Why don't we head out and go for a drive. We can see if we can find Mia or maybe someone that might know him. We can also check the old warehouse that you lived in, perhaps he went back there," Alex offered.

I hadn't even thought about the warehouse. If Mia was hurt or high, he might have gone there instead of coming home. I gave a nod and we headed out. I was hoping and praying that we would find Mia and that he was okay. I just needed him to be okay, because if he wasn't, I had no idea what I would do.

CHAPTER EIGHTEEN

Eli

"STOP FIGHTING AGAINST us, Eli. You are infected. You have a disease and the only way to rid yourself of it is by accepting the pain."

My screams echoed off of the walls within the cold room. I had been tied to this chair many times, but today was different. They were forcing me to watch gay porn and whenever I got hard, I was electrocuted by a cattle prod to my genitals. The pain was excruciating and there was nothing I could do to stop it. I couldn't control how my body reacted to the sounds and images coming from the screen. Just like I couldn't control the tears that freely rolled down my cheeks at the harsh and degrading words that were spoken to me.

I wanted this to stop.

I wanted to go home.

I didn't really have a home, but it was better than this.

The pain was back and once again I had to fight with consciousness as my body was rocked with pain.

I wanted this to end.

I had already made a plan on how I could end my life tonight.

HIDDEN

I just needed to survive this torture so I could finally go to sleep and never feel anything ever again.

"Eli, Sweetheart, wake up."

That voice was different and it didn't belong here. I couldn't figure out where the voice was coming from.

All I could feel was pain.

"Baby, I need you to wake up. Come on, Sweetheart, open your eyes for me."

That voice wouldn't stop and I couldn't figure out where it was coming from. I could feel my body shaking, I didn't know what was happening, but just as the cattle prod got closer the room disappeared.

I sat up in bed, breathing heavily. I scanned the room and I fought to recognize where I was. I was no longer in that cold room at the camp, but instead,

I sat on a soft bed in a warm room. At the feeling of hands on my arms, I jumped and turned to see who had touched me.

"It's okay, Sweetheart. It's okay, it's just me," Alex said gently as he held his hands up.

I closed my eyes and tried to catch my breath, but it was not that simple. My whole body was shaking and I was having a very hard time regulating my breathing back to normal. I felt the bed move and I could hear Alex moving around. I tried my best to get my body to listen to me, but it just wouldn't.

I opened my eyes when I felt a heavy weight against my legs and I saw that Alex had pulled out the weighted blanket he got for me. I had yet to use it because I hadn't needed it this past week. Once the blanket was on me, Alex was back in bed and I leaned against him. He lay down and I instantly curled up against his chest. The feel of his arms wrapped around me and the weight of the blanket, I could feel my breathing getting back to normal.

"You're okay. It was just a nightmare, Sweetheart."

"It felt so real, like I was back there," I said as the tears started to build in the corners of my eyes.

I knew what triggered this nightmare. We hadn't found Mia today and Roland didn't sound hopeful when we spoke to him earlier. We had searched the whole city, but we didn't find any trace of Mia.

"I know, but you're not there. You are safe, here, in your own bed, in your own apartment. You're safe, Sweetheart,"

Alex said. He placed a kiss on the top of my head. "Talk to me, it'll help."

The very last thing I wanted to do was to talk about it, but I knew he was right.

"It was the day I met Mia. They had me in that room, they liked to force me to watch gay porn and whenever I got hard they would electrocute me with a cattle prod to my genitals. The pain was unbearable and I couldn't do it anymore. I had already made a plan that night to kill myself. Only, when I was about to do it, the door opened and they pushed Mia into the room. The guards didn't notice, but he did. He didn't say anything about it, though. He just sat down on the bed next to me and he talked. He talked about nothing all night long and come morning, I knew I had to keep going so I could be there for him. He saved my life."

HIDDEN

I had never told anyone about that night. I had no one to tell. I had no idea how Alex was going to feel about my admitting I had wanted to kill myself. Maybe it wouldn't be that surprising considering everything I had been going through in the camp. He was also a shrink, so it couldn't be the first time he had heard someone admit to wanting to die. Still, it made me feel weak and I hated being weak around him.

"I'm glad he did. What you and Mia have is such a strong bond and I know that will be what makes Mia come back, what helps him to start to heal from everything that happened to him. It's natural, though, Eli, that you would have wanted to end your suffering. You had been there for years. It is only natural that you would reach a breaking point. You are not the only survivor of the camp that has thought about it, or has tried it. Just like there would have been others that did kill themselves while in the camp. Anyone would feel that way after going through the hell you were trapped in."

Hearing how sweet and understanding he was being with me was what started the tears to roll down my cheeks. I didn't deserve this man.

"You don't deserve to be going through this. You don't deserve to be trapped with my screwed up mind," I said through the tears.

"You are not screwed up, Sweetheart. You're hurt and sick, but that doesn't make you worthless or screwed up. You have PTSD, but you are fighting every day to get better. You are so incredibly strong, Eli, and I couldn't be more proud of you. You are a wonderful and caring man, and I can't wait to watch you continue to grow. You are going to change this world, and I am going to be right there beside you as you do. I'm not going anywhere, Sweetheart."

I turned my face into his chest and allowed the tears to flow freely.

To cry out the pain of the nightmare.

To cry out the pain and uncertainty of Mia's disappearance.

To cry out all of the feelings of unworthiness.

Through it all, Alex continued to hold me and tell me that he was always going to be with me. For the first time in my life, I believed that I wouldn't have to go through all of this alone. I had Alex and, for the first time, there was a small light at the end of this very dark tunnel.

CHAPTER NINETEEN

Alex

IT HAD BEEN a week since Eli had called me to inform me that Mia was missing. For the past week, Eli had been a complete mess.

I had hoped that Sebastian would have been able to find Mia long before now, but so far he was a ghost. We had phoned the police and filed a report, but they weren't too interested in finding him. To them, Mia was a prostitute and eighteen. He was an adult. It made him a low priority, which I understood, but Eli was having a very hard time with accepting that his brother was out there on his own. Roland was looking into it, as well, but he also still had his hands full with the camp victims and he was occasionally helping with the task force that his brother was running.

As a psychiatrist, I knew what Mia was doing. It wasn't that unexpected to me. He had been through something traumatic from being in the camp and that was causing him problems. Just like that trauma was causing Eli problems. The difference was how they were both responding to that trauma. Eli was there longer and it had given him

PTSD. Whereas Mia had a whole childhood of trauma and he was reacting to it through promiscuity and getting involved in the wrong crowd.

We were reasonably sure, now, that he had a pimp, and it was not going to be as simple as moving to get him away from that authority. There were deep psychological issues that needed to be dealt with if Mia was going to have a true chance of starting fresh. Unfortunately, until Mia was ready, there was nothing any of us could do for him. All I could do was try and keep Eli from breaking down.

That breakdown was coming, I could see it, and that was what I was worried about the most. I had no idea what Eli would be like when his mind finally gave out on him. He had been doing so well, remarkably well, and I knew he didn't want to lose what he had gained.

He was still going to work, despite not feeling himself. He was struggling, but he was trying to keep moving forward. We would need to have the conversation about him living his life for himself regardless of what Mia does. It was not going to be an easy conversation, but it was one we needed to have.

That conversation should really occur with his own psychiatrist, but Dr. Bailey hadn't shown any interest in meeting with Eli. I knew he called her when Mia went missing, but she didn't even bother calling him back. It was completely unprofessional and ridiculous. If she was not going to be there for Eli and help him through his trauma, then I needed to be there for him.

I had been trying to walk a fine line between being his doctor and being his boyfriend. However, given that Dr. Bailey had zero interest in being Eli's doctor, that responsibility was falling on my shoulders.

I looked up when someone sat across from me. I had left my office to come and work a bit at the cafe. My annoyance level began to increase once I saw that it was Dr. Bailey who sat down across from me. Based on her expression, I apparently wasn't the only one annoyed by this meeting.

"Heather, what can I do for you?" I asked, not looking to drag this out any.

"I wasn't aware you were hurting for clients, Alex. You should have called, I might have been able to give you some of my more undesirable ones."

I knew what she was getting at. She'd most likely discovered that I was spending a good amount of time with Eli. It wouldn't be hard for her to discover the information. We shared a meal together at the diner five days a week. I was always there to spend Eli's lunch or dinner break with him. Plus, we were often out together going to see a movie or to grab some coffee. This was a small town and people talked.

In this case, people would likely believe I was giving therapy to Eli with my profession over us being in a romantic relationship. It was a good cover, because I was not sure if Eli wanted people to know about us or was ready to have a public relationship. He was going through a lot and it would only make sense why he needed time before going public with our relationship.

"There is no such thing as undesirable patients, Heather. Though, you and I have never seen eye to eye where that topic was concerned."

She was clearly not impressed by me calling her out on that. She knew we were different from each other in how we practiced and treated our patients.

She preferred to have easy, rich clients who were there because their parents demanded it. She wanted nothing to do with patients that actually needed the support and help. She made a great deal of money and I knew that was what she wanted. She became a psychiatrist for the payout.

Whereas I became a psychiatrist to help people. I wanted to help those that couldn't afford to pay me. I wanted to take on as many pro bono cases as I could, because they were the people that desperately needed the help.

Especially children.

They are the ones that need the most help and they shouldn't have to be punished because they didn't have parents that were able to afford proper therapy. If I had never met Eli, he would still be one of those young adults left to drown in their own mental health issues.

"Some people are damaged beyond belief and they will never get better. It's a waste of time to try and entertain that they could be healed. The best thing for them is to prescribe them medication and let nature take its course. Natural selection is indeed real, Alex, even if you refuse to believe it."

"And you think Eli deserves to be a part of that natural selection? He's an eighteen year old man who went through years of trauma, of torture. He has PTSD and even someone as blind as you should be able to see that. He needs support and help so he can have a normal life. He doesn't need to be kept numb by medication."

I was doing my best to keep my voice calm, but it was becoming difficult the more this conversation continued. I was not going to allow anyone to talk crap about Eli. He was trying his damn best to function in this world. He was trying to have a life after his was robbed from him. After his childhood was robbed from him. Eli had no one to protect him growing up and I would be damned if I was going to allow Eli to be unprotected.

"PTSD is incurable. All you are doing is delaying the inevitable. Eli is a lost cause, just like everyone else with PTSD. There's no money to be made from lost causes. Just because I am glad to see that Eli is no longer going to be my patient, that does not change the fact that I don't appreciate you stealing one of my patients. You are lucky that it was not a high paying patient," Dr. Bailey lightly threatened.

The thing was, I would never steal a patient from anyone, much less one of Dr. Bailey's. All of her patients that were higher paying, didn't really need therapy. They were simply there because their parents felt like they were being rebellious or they were refusing to live a life that their parents forced them to have. No. They didn't need therapy. They needed to be eighteen so they could move away from their parents and the control.

"I didn't steal a patient from you, Heather. Eli is not my patient. He is a friend. If he has chosen to no longer see you, that is his choice. It has nothing to do with me."

That wasn't fully true, but she didn't need to know that. She didn't need to know what my personal relationship was with Eli.

I packed up my laptop and stood. I was not about to keep having this conversation with her. I had come here to work and now I was, once again, interrupted. Today seemed like it was going to be a bust where my paperwork was concerned. I headed out, not even bothering with saying goodbye. Dr.

Bailey would never understand my perspective and there was no point in trying to get her to.

Just as I got into my car, my phone trilled. I pulled it out of my pocket and saw that it was Zane.

"Hello," I answered.

"Hey, Alex. I just wanted to check in and make sure that Eli was okay. Jimmy told me he called in sick today," Zane said, concern lacing his voice.

That was news to me, though it wasn't that unexpected. Eli had been going down a very slippery slope since Mia had turned up missing. It was only a matter of time before he hit the bottom.

"He's recovering. I am sure you've heard that Mia is missing, has been for a week. Eli is trying to keep it all together.

I'm sure all of the stress and worry has taken on a physical ailment." I didn't want to make it seem like Eli couldn't handle doing his job. The very last thing I wanted was to cost Eli his job.

"I've heard. We've been helping Roland try to find him at night. We haven't found any trace of him. Roland thinks he might have skipped town to avoid being found. I'm really sorry for Eli. I know him and Mia are brothers. I called him, but Eli didn't answer. When you see him next, could you please let him know he can have all the time off that he needs."

"I appreciate that, and I will let him know when I go and see him later. I appreciate you helping to try and find Mia. He's been through a lot and I hate to think that he is out there on his own."

That was what bothered me the most. Knowing that Mia was out there all on his own going through who knows what, and I knew that was bothering Eli as well. If we could see him, and check in on him, it would be easier to deal with. We would at least know where he was living. As it stands, we had no idea what town he's even in. The unknown was going to destroy Eli if I didn't do something to stop it.

"We're always here for the both of you, should either of you wish to talk."

"I appreciate that, Zane. I'll go and check in on Eli and make sure he is okay."

"Let me know if you need any help with him."

"I will. Thank you."

After saying a quick goodbye, I

shoved my phone back into my pocket and twisted the key in the ignition. Pulling out into traffic, I headed off for Eli's new place and hoped he wouldn't be too rough when I got there.

Ten minutes later, I was walking through his door. The lights were off so I made my way toward Eli's bedroom. He was in there with the door closed and the lights were off there, too. I made my way over to the bedside table and clicked on the light as I spoke.

"Sweetheart."

Once there was some light in the room, I could see that Eli wasn't sleeping. He was curled up on his right side facing the door. The whites of his eyes were red, the sockets swollen and puffy, and I knew he had been crying. He looked exhausted. He had been exhausted for a week, now. He was barely sleeping and it was concerning, because he needed proper sleep to keep his PTSD at bay.

"Hey," Eli said, softly.

"Having a bad day today?" I asked, gently.

"Yeah."

"And that's okay. You are going to have bad days, and when they come up, you are doing exactly what you need to be doing to get through them and back on track. You take the day for yourself and rest so you can tackle the world tomorrow," I said as I ran my hand through his hair.

"I don't know if I can do this. He's just out there, all alone. He could be dead and I wouldn't even know it," Eli said as the tears started to build up in his eyes.

"I wish I could take this pain away from you. I would do it in a second, if I could. I know this isn't easy and I'm going to tell you something that you are not going to want to do. But, Sweetheart, you can't live your life for Mia. You can't stand still and wait for him to come back. You have to keep moving forward. You have to keep living your life. The only way you are going to be able to help Mia when he comes back, is to help yourself right now. You need to rest and you need to get stronger and healthier. That is the only way you are going to be able to help Mia."

I knew what I was asking him would be a Herculean task for him, especially right now. But I wanted him to start thinking about his future and how he was going to live his life. He couldn't live it for anyone else but himself.

"I can't just leave him behind."

"You're not, Sweetheart. You are choosing to be ready for when he does come back. He's going to need help and the only way you can help him is if you are healthy enough to. Choosing to live your life, choosing to keep working on your mental health, is not choosing to forget about Mia. It's you trying to be the best version of yourself so you can help Mia when we find him."

I needed to get Eli to see that by helping himself, he would be putting himself into a better position to help Mia. He couldn't help Mia when he was like this. He had to get better. He had to get stronger mentally so he could be able to handle whatever problems came with

Mia.

Eli couldn't keep the tears at bay any longer as he gave me a nod of understanding. I quickly removed my shoes and coat before I went around and got into the bed. I wrapped my arms around him and kissed the back of his neck.

"It's okay, Sweetheart."

I knew there was nothing else I would be able to say to him. He had to cry this pain out and then, hopefully, tomorrow he would be in better shape. We had to keep moving forward, no matter how much it hurt. Mia would be found, eventually. He would either show up or he would be arrested for prostitution. Either way, Eli would be reunited with Mia one day and I was going to make sure he was ready for when that happened.

EPILOGUE

Eli

"ARE YOU SURE she doesn't need to be at the vet?" I asked as we both sat there watching Lucy.

The dog was currently in labor and I felt very nervous and concerned for her. Alex seemed to be perfectly calm with everything going on with her. I had no idea how he could be this calm.

She was in labor, had been for four hours now, and I was a wreck over it.

Alex had told me she would be fine. That she didn't need to go to the vet, but I couldn't help but feel like it would be safer for her. When a woman goes into labor, she goes straight to the hospital where doctors and nurses are there to help her through it. To make sure that her baby is okay. And that was typically for one baby.

Lucy was having a whole liter of them.

"She's okay. Normally, animals don't have to go to the vet when they are in labor. If she doesn't give birth within the next twelve hours, then we'll take her. I promise you, she's okay. She'll do what she needs to do to get her babies out."

"When do they have to go to the

charity?" I asked.

I knew that Alex was planning on sending the puppies to a service dog charity that would pair them up with someone in need of a service dog. I just wasn't sure on how it all worked.

"When they are eight weeks old, then they will be weaned from Lucy and they will go to the charity. I'm keeping one of the females for Lucy. I also want you to keep one."

"What?" I asked, confused. This was the first time he had mentioned anything about me keeping a puppy.

"When they are eight weeks old, I want you to pick one to keep for yourself. I know we hadn't talked about it, but I think it would be really good for you to have a service dog. You've been doing so well in the past few months and

I think having a service dog would be amazing for you. The charity is even offering training completely free to any of the camp survivors with a doctor's note that specifies the need for a service dog. I can easily give you one. The choice is obviously yours, Sweetheart, but it's something for you to think about."

I had never thought about having a dog for my PTSD. I had always wanted a dog and I thought maybe one day I would get one. Having Lucy around me had really solidified my desire for a dog. I just never thought I would have one as a service dog. I wasn't too sure what a service dog would do for me, though. I knew that there were plenty of people with a service dog that helped them with anxiety and PTSD, I just didn't understand *how*. It was something to think about, though, and do some research. I had eight weeks before I would need to decide.

"I'll think about it," I promised.

"That's all I ask." he said, flashing me a warm smile.

I couldn't believe he was still here.

I never thought I would ever have the chance to be with a man ever again. I never thought I would want to be with someone after what the camp did to me. I thought I was broken. I thought I was unrepairable and doomed to be homeless for the rest of my life.

Since I had known Alex, I had been able to get better control over my anxiety. I had been able to enjoy being with a man again. I never thought I would ever be able to feel pleasure again, but Alex had shown me that I could.

It had been almost two months since Mia had gone missing. I thought it would break me, but Alex refused to allow it. He allowed me to feel depressed and hurt over Mia's disappearance. However, he also made sure I felt loved and strong. He never allowed me to give up, even when everything in me was screaming to do just that.

I could have lost everything that I had been fighting to obtain since being free from my hell. Thanks to Alex, I felt alive again, perhaps for the first time in my life.

I had fallen in love with him, too.

I had no idea how it happened, it all still felt like a dream to me. I keep waiting to wake up only to discover these past few months had never happened. That I was still trapped in that camp and no one was going to come and rescue me.

It was surreal when I thought about how far I had come. I never expected it and I knew I had a long way to go. I knew there were plenty of hard days ahead of me. However, I also knew that I could handle them. With Alex by my side, I could handle anything that came my way.

So far, I hadn't heard anything about Mia. Everyone within our circle had looked all over the town for him multiple times, but we'd never found him. We hadn't even found anyone that had seen him recently.

My worst fears had been confirmed at that point, that Mia was no longer in town. He had left, and what scared me most was that I knew in my gut he had been forced to leave by his pimp. I had no idea who his pimp was, but I knew it wasn't anyone good.

I had no idea how I was ever going to find him.

Roland said he would know if Mia was arrested, and Sebastian had promised to keep looking for him using his connections. Unfortunately, until he popped up there was nothing I could do for him. I hated feeling useless, but there was literally nothing I could do. I couldn't go out there and start traveling from city to city trying to find him. That wasn't healthy, nor was it feasible. I had a job here, an apartment. I had to live my life and hope that Mia would be back soon.

It was hard, at first, living my life without him. We had spent so long in that camp relying on each other that being without him was very hard. I was so used to seeing him every day. To always be able to talk to him and work through problems. For the first time in a long time, I had to go through life without him and it made it harder, but I had held on. Alex had shown me that I wasn't alone. I had a whole family out there for me.

I finally had a true family.

I was finally safe and loved.

It was all a dream come true and I owed it all to Alex.

***

I was never going to get tired of the feel of Alex's lips against my skin.

We had migrated to his bedroom now that Lucy had given birth and all of the puppies were sleeping. They were ridiculously cute and I already was falling in love with one of the males. When Alex had suggested me keeping one, I wasn't too certain, but it was love at first sight with that little puppy. I knew I would need to keep him and I already couldn't wait to see him grow up.

Over the past couple of months, we had been slowly taking things further with our sexual relationship. However, we had yet to have sex. Alex knew I was a virgin and he was respecting my pace. I loved him for that, but tonight I didn't want to stop. I wanted to feel him inside of me and I was really hoping he wouldn't say no. When we broke apart from the kiss, I spoke.

"I want you."

"Are you sure?" Alex asked, but I

could tell he really wanted me as well and that only solidified my need.

"Fuck yes."

That was all Alex needed before his lips were crushing against mine. We were already naked and he was on top of me. The both of us were painfully hard and we needed to find some release soon.

Alex's tongue dominated my mouth as he reached over to grab the lube he kept in the bedside drawer. We had spoken about this before and we had both agreed that condoms weren't needed. I had been clean and Alex had tested clean as well. I wanted my first time to be with Alex and I wanted to feel his skin inside of me and not latex.

Alex kissed his way down my body until he reached my dick. He instantly took me into his mouth all the way down to the base. I gave a deep moan as the heat surrounded my sensitive dick.

He used the distraction to slowly insert a lubed up finger inside of me. I was used to it, though, because we had done this before. We never took it further, but this was not the first time Alex had fingered me.

I easily relaxed as Alex worked my hole. He added a second and then a third finger when he felt me ready, and the second he hit my sweet spot I saw stars. It didn't take long before I gave him a long and deep moan as I came hard into his mouth. Alex moaned his appreciation as he swallowed everything I had for him and once I stopped pulsing, he pulled his mouth off me and his fingers out of me. He spoke as he grabbed the lube to slick himself up.

"You sure, Sweetheart?"

"More than I have ever been in my life," I replied easily and flashed him a seductive smile.

I wanted him.

I wanted Alex to be my first.

Hell, I wanted him to be my last.

I loved this man and I never wanted to be without him. I wanted the connection that this would bring us and it would be the very last thing that I was taking back after the camp. They thought they could break me, but they were wrong.

So very wrong.

Alex leaned down and started to kiss mc slowly. I easily welcomed his tongue as I felt the tip of his dick against my hole.

I relaxed my body and focused on Alex's magical mouth as he slowly pushed into me. I knew there would be a burn and a slight sting. Alex had stretched me, but there was only so much stretching you could do with your fingers. However, I knew it would feel good soon enough, just like his fingers had.

Alex went slow. Inch by inch, he pushed inside of me until he was down to his base. Once he was all the way inside of me, he broke from the kiss so he could try and catch his breath. I could tell he wanted to move, but he was allowing my body the time it needed to adjust to his size. He was big, but he felt amazing. I felt like we were connected fully, that our bodies were becoming one, and it felt truly remarkable.

"I'm okay, you can move," I said after a moment.

Alex pulled out almost all of the way before he slowly pushed back in and groaned. "You feel so good, Sweetheart."

"Oh god, you feel amazing," I moaned as my body started to loosen up and adjust to his size.

Once my body was loosened up enough, he started to pick up his pace. I wrapped my legs around his hips and easily met his thrusts with my hips. I couldn't stop moaning. My whole body felt amazing. There was a tingle going through it and I never wanted this to end.

I could tell Alex was getting close as his thrusts started to become more erratic. I angled my hips and with that slight adjustment, his tip hit my sweet spot dead on and I saw stars.

"Fuck, don't stop. I'm so close, Baby," I moaned out on a heavy breath as I could feel my own release approaching once again.

"Come for me, Sweetheart. I want to feel your sweet, tight ass come around my cock," Alex said as he pounded harder into me.

My whole body was shaking from the pleasure. I had no idea I could ever feel this good in my life. I could easily become addicted to this, addicted to Alex and his body.

Alex snaked his hand around and started to jerk me off in time with his thrusts and only a moment later my back was arching as I came hard once again.

The added tightness of my ass as I

clamped around his dick was enough to push Alex over the edge and I continued to throb and pulse as I felt the heat of his cum hitting my inner walls. I was never going to get tired of that feeling.

We were both breathing heavily as our bodies continued to pulse from the life altering pleasure we had just experienced. My legs lost all strength and I let them collapse down onto the bed as I fought for breath. Alex had recovered a bit faster than me and he started to kiss along my neck.

"I love you," he said.

He had never said those words to me before and instantly, a deep warmth filled my chest. I had fallen in love with him a month prior, but I had been terrified to say anything first. I had no idea if he was feeling the same as me and I was not about to risk losing him by saying the words first.

"I love you, too," I easily said back.

Alex lightly kissed my lips and we lay quietly, enjoying the other's body being connected to ours. We lightly kissed, and I lightly trailed my fingertips through the hair on his chest as we allowed our breathing to return to normal. Alex pulled back after a good ten minutes and he gave me a very sexy smile as he looked down at me.

"I am nowhere near done with you tonight, Sweetheart."

A huge smile instantly hit my face. That was a promise I was more than happy to allow him to keep. I had no idea what the future held for us, but I knew whatever it was, it was going to be amazing. I had escaped from the camp and I was finally going to get to live my dreams with the most amazing man by my side.

Thank you for reading Hidden, book five in the From the Edge series!

If you enjoyed Hidden, please return to your retailer and leave a review. Even a few words can mean the world to an author. Plus it helps other readers like you find our work, too.
Share the love! ;)

Turn the page to read a preview from Tormented, the next book in the series.

PREVIEW

Isaiah

I LET OUT a sigh as I looked at the mess of paperwork that was currently spread all across my dining room table. I knew when I accepted the position that working for the task force I was going to have a great deal of work ahead of me. However, I knew it would be worth it to help children in need. I just never expected for it to be this hard, for it to hit this close to home.

The task force had been working with the local authorities just five hundred miles from town. They were made aware of a Fundamentalist Church of Jesus Christ of Latter-Day Saints, FLDS, stronghold where they sent children they deemed were in need of repenting. The compound was heavily guarded with FLDS security that used military grade weapons. We still weren't sure how they got a hold of the regulated weapons. The team was trying to look into it and track down how they received the weapons.

Like all takedown operations that involved children, I went with the team to the FLDS stronghold. I stayed back in the van until the area had been cleared and secured. For most, it wouldn't have been a big deal to go into the stronghold and see the children. However, for me, I knew exactly what to expect within the compound.

I had been one of the unfortunate children born into the FLDS. My mother was my father's eighteenth wife and she was only twelve when they got married. The Prophet had told my father that he needed more wives to produce more children for him to be allowed to enter the Golden Kingdom when he died. The problem was, there were only so many women old enough to legally be married.

Not that they really got married.

Anyone after the first wife was purely a spiritual wife. Still, the amount of single females over the age of eighteen dwindled down drastically over the years. My mother was fourteen when she gave birth to me and I am one of twenty-eight siblings.

For the first eighteen years of my life, I dealt with being abused and neglected by my father and my mother. My father, I would only see him once or twice a year. He was always too busy with his other wives or working to truly pay any attention to us. My mother was too broken by my father to take care of us. She had ten children, nine after me, and by that point she had lost all traces of her own identity. She spent her days looking out the window, waiting for when my father would walk up the path.

With my mother being checked out, everything rested on my shoulders.

We all lived in homes that should have been condemned. There was no running water, no electricity, and there were only three bedrooms, leaving five kids in a room. The rooms weren't even big enough for proper beds. We all slept together on the floor, on a king size mattress.

There was no such thing as personal space.

There was no such thing as privacy.

The single bathroom in the house barely worked and we often had to go out into the woods to use the bathroom. We rarely got to shower and get clean. We used to have to use rain barrels and hope we would have enough water to get clean once a week.

The place was always dirty, despite the amount of hours I would spend cleaning it. We had cockroaches and mice running all over the place. You would be sleeping and get bitten by something and have no idea what it was.

The food we would get was always just about rotten or already rotten. It was all we could afford with the very miniscule amount of money that we got from my father. It was up to me to cook and as I got older, I got more creative with the food. I had been able to come up with different meals to make with the same food. My siblings appreciated it, and it made me feel good to see the pleasure on their faces at the delicious taste.

It was then that I discovered my love of cooking. I loved knowing that I could make someone happy by just eating my food. It encouraged me to try different things and to see what else I could come up with and my siblings never said no to trying something I cooked.

HIDDEN

Within the FLDS, children were home schooled or taught by the church and it was never anything that would be recognized by the State as proper schooling.

I would sneak out and learn down at the community center. I had to be careful and keep it hidden, because if I had been caught I would have been sent to the reform camp to repent for my sins, leaving my siblings to fend for themselves.

Problems had come up over the years before I turned eighteen. The most common was my father pressuring me to find a wife, or my father trying to set one of my younger sisters up with a husband.

When I turned eighteen, I had my escape plan ready.

No one could just leave the FLDS. They ruled with intimidation and abuse. I had already experienced it enough from my father and my uncles over the eighteen years of being trapped there.

I had tried to get all of my siblings to leave with me, but I could only get five of them to agree to leave. I was okay with that, though, because the five that I did get were my sisters. They were my full-blooded sisters and despite not being able to get my half-sisters, I knew that getting five of them out with me was more than I could have hoped for. They were all underage and that made it very difficult and, technically, I committed five counts of kidnapping that I could still be charged with to this day should it ever get out.

Still, I had never regretted it for a

single second.

That night, I'd had everything planned.

We had all packed a bag so we were ready. My sisters all shared a room so I didn't have to worry about anyone spotting them leaving. With me being eighteen, I was free to leave the house should I wish.

I had said goodbye to my brothers and got the girls out through their bedroom window. We had to walk through the dark ten miles to a car that was waiting for us. I had reached out to a woman that helped FLDS members to escape the cult. She knew to be prepared for six of us, but I had neglected to inform her of my sisters' ages. She wasn't happy, but she was not about to turn them away. She knew all too well what fate awaited them back at the compound.

We drove out of state into Nevada, adding more charges against me, until we arrived at my aunt's home. She had gotten out when she was twenty and had space for us to hide out. Once we arrived, my aunt was already set to take all of us in.

Our saving grace was that Nevada was a safe haven state. Even if the police caught us, they would never send my siblings back to my parents. We would be able to get sanctuary for them and that was all that I cared about.

I had only stayed for two months in the summer before I was off to College. I wanted to get my Masters in Social Work so I would be able to help save more children like my siblings. Now, fifteen years later, my sisters were still living their lives free from the FLDS, and I worked for a Federal Task Force helping to stop crimes against children.

The loud trill of my phone ringing pulled me out of my reminiscing thoughts and I glanced at the screen, noting it was Travis Manning calling. Travis was another social worker helping with the task force and we had become very good friends.

I had been worried about Travis recently, though, because he'd been acting differently. I had seen a couple of bruises on him, too, but he had dismissed them as it being a result of a self-defense class.

I could tell he wasn't telling me the full truth, right away.

Travis had a tell when he was lying,

he always looked away slightly. He was such a good man that he couldn't look someone in the eye and lie to them. I knew that I couldn't help him until he was ready to ask for help. I just hoped that whatever was going on, it was something that he could survive.

"Hey, Travis, you working late, too?" I asked as I answered the phone.

"The one hundred and five case files currently sitting on my floor have decided sleep is for the weak," he joked lightly.

"I know. When I agreed to being on the task force as a social worker, I didn't expect to have this much paperwork. Nor this many cases of children I needed to place. We're running out of foster homes."

That was my biggest concern.

The task force had federal clearance so they could go all over the country to work any cases and chase after any criminal. It was great because it allowed them to get the worst criminals against children off the streets and either in jail or in the ground.

The problem was, though, the children that were left behind after these cases. Some could be placed in foster homes locally, but there were also children that needed a place to go until we could find their family. We had a lot of children stuck in a transition position because we were trying to track down a next of kin for them.

Or they were seventeen and only had months left. We didn't want a bunch of newly eighteen years olds being homeless on the streets, so we were trying to find a place for them to go.

In town, we had a motel that gave us a weekly voucher for the homeless or newly aged out foster kids that needed a place to stay for a week or so until they could get on their feet. However, it wasn't enough for the kids that needed more than a week. We had to find another solution and that also rested on our shoulders.

"I know, that is why I have spoken with Dominic O'Conner. He is new in town and has purchased the Capitol building. That's where Eli is currently living. Dom has expressed interest in helping the children. He had a good size settlement from the death of his son and has been investing it to generate more capital. I thought I could set up a meeting between the two of you and maybe you could come up with some sort of longer term solution."

If we had even one person who would invest in helping financially with a new group home of sorts, that could help. We would need to find other investors for it to be sustainable, but if we had the connection of getting started with Dominic, that could be what we need to get a group home up and running.

"Okay, set it up and I'll see what I can do."

"I'll reach out to him tomorrow. We gotta do something before the foster homes get too many children and we risk them being neglected or abused."

"No, I agree, something has to give before the system breaks more than it already is. We are finally getting the system back together, I don't want it to slip and go back to how it used to be."

"We'll get it worked out. Now, tell me, what are you eating?" Travis asked, and I could hear the smile in his voice.

Everyone knew I liked food. That was not that surprising considering I was above average in terms of body weight. I wasn't overweight, but I did have a Dad Bod.

After growing up barely being able to eat, when I turned eighteen and had money for proper food, I tended to eat quite a bit. At first, I burned through it easily enough, but as I got older my metabolism slowed down and it got harder for me to lose the weight.

Cooking had also become something that brought me comfort and stress relief. Whenever I was feeling stressed or upset, I would cook something. It helped to calm me down and it made me feel better. Dr. Holland, the psychologist at work, had informed me that it wasn't the worst coping mechanism out there. I wasn't drinking or doing drugs to relieve the stress. I knew what he wasn't saying, though. Eventually, I would be putting my health at risk, all the same. If I gained too much weight, I was looking at high blood pressure, diabetes, and high cholesterol. None of which would be good and could do the same damage that drinking or drugs would do to my body. I knew I needed to try and find a way to lose some weight or to cook less, but I didn't have the drive for that, currently.

"Just some leftover chicken alfredo pasta that I made before we had to head out. It's nothing fancy, but I had a new recipe to cook it in a slow cooker."

"Sounds good. How is it?"

"It's good. Anything I can make in a slow cooker, I am happy to try."

"Same, I have to get a new slow cooker because I have used mine so much it's dead now."

I could understand that all too well. With our jobs, it is rarely nine to five and we are often stuck at the office working late. A slow cooker allowed us to work any number of hours and come home to a freshly cooked meal. It was a huge saving grace in my life and I was always looking for unique recipes for it.

"I just got a new one on sale before we got hit with this case. It was only thirty bucks and it holds enough for six people," I supplied.

"Shit, I gotta get me one. I'll go out and grab it tomorrow. I don't need to eat that much, but I like to make a huge batch and freeze it."

"Absolutely. I do that all the time. It makes life so much easier," I easily agreed.

"I'll let you go so you can get back to work. Or we both can, I should say. I'll see you tomorrow."

"Always. Good night, Travis."

"Goodnight."

I ended the call and placed my phone back down on the table. I let out a sigh as I looked at all of the case folders that were covering my table. I had a long night ahead of me, but I knew I would never make it through all of this work in one night. I would stay up for a couple more hours before I headed off to bed to get six hours of sleep. Tomorrow, I would get back to finding these children safe homes and, hopefully, they would no longer have to live in fear.

Watch for Tormented at your favorite online retailer.

OTHER BOOKS BY EVIE

Federal Protection Agency
Mason
Rafe
Ryzen
Cooper
Noah
Damien
Sebastian
Gabe
Logan

Ruthless Empire
Courting Danger
Chasing Danger
Kissing Danger

Smokejumpers
Hawke
Cyrus
Jase
Gage
Jackson
Xavier

Jasper Springs
Cade
Dawson
Drew
Grayson
Riley
Mitch

From The Edge
Shattered
Runaway
Jaded
Rescue
Hidden
Tormented

Gray Vale Pack
His Fated Mate
His Wounded Warrior
His Healing Heart

ABOUT THE AUTHOR

Evie Riley is a prolific, neurodivergent author known for her captivating MM romance novels. She has gained a significant following and topped the LGBT+ action and adventure bestseller charts with her series.

Evie's writing style often explores dark and gritty themes where her men must overcome difficult obstacles in their search for love, but she has also ventured into sweeter small-town romances, incorporating tropes like enemies-to-lovers, friends-to-lovers, age-gap, and forced proximity. She is known for crafting engaging romantic suspense novels and has a knack for creating interconnected series worlds that keep readers invested.

Interestingly, Ms. Riley has hinted at exploring new genres, such as Alien Omegaverse Romance, in the future.

Outside of writing, she enjoys spending time at the beach and has a quirky personality, described by her partner as ranging from cute to deadly, depending on her blood-chocolate levels.

Evie spends her nights writing bad boys in love, and her days wrangling the sweet boys she loves.